DATE DUE

DATE DUE

The Falcon

The Falcon

Jackie French Koller

Atheneum Books for Young Readers

The poem "The Falcon" by Ryan Koller is used with the author's permission.

Atheneum Books for Young Readers
An imprint of Simon & Schuster Children's Publishing Division
1230 Avenue of the Americas
New York, New York 10020

Book design by Angela Carlino
The text of this book is set in Baskerville BE

First Edition
Printed in the United States of America
10 9 8 7 6 5 4 3 2

Library of Congress Cataloging-in-Publication Data
Koller, Jackie French.
The Falcon / by Jackie French Koller.–1st ed.
p. cm.
Summary: While running from the truth to escape painful memories of losing his eye,
seventeen-year-old Luke gets himself into a series of dangerous situations.
ISBN 0-689-81294-9
[1. Honesty–Fiction.] I. Title.
PZ7.K844Fal 1998
[Fic]–dc21
97-34062
CIP AC

To Ana, who helps me see the forest through the trees

Writers are great eavesdroppers, who regularly mine the lives of their friends and family members in search of story ideas. I wish to thank my son, Ryan, for allowing me to borrow from certain events in his life to create Luke's story, and I want to make it perfectly clear that, despite some obvious similarities between Luke and Ryan, *The Falcon* is a work of fiction, not in any way to be misconstrued as factual or biographical.

The Falcon

Sunday, January 5

~~This is the journal of Luke~~
~~Carver, age 17.~~

I, Luke Carver, hereby
start my journal.

Dear Journal,

Sunday, January 5

This is the journal of Luke Carver, age 17.

I, Luke Carver, hereby start my journal.

Dear Journal,

Man, is this lame or what? A seventeen-year-old guy writing a journal. I don't even know how to start. The whole thing is Mrs. Robinson's idea. She's making us write a practice essay for our college applications at the end of this quarter, because we have to write one for real next fall when we're seniors. She's making a big deal out of it because she says it's getting harder and harder to get into college, and colleges are even more interested in essays these days than in the SATs. So, anyhow, she came up with this journal idea. She says lots of real writers keep journals and that they're a good way to get to know yourself and to sort out what's important to you and stuff like that. Sounds like a chick thing to me, but she swears guys do it, too. Anyhow, she's going to check them every day—not actually read them—but just see how much we've written, so I guess I better write something. Trouble is, I've kind of procrastinated again. I was supposed to be writing in it all during Christmas break, and now, here it is, the night before school starts again, and I'm just starting. Oh well. Maybe if I write a whole bunch at once she won't notice.

Hey, half a page already. Not bad. Okay, so what else do I feel like writing about? Nothing to do with any college essay, that's for sure. Mrs. Robinson said we should just write about whatever we're thinking about, but all I keep thinking about is my girlfriend, Megan, and how pretty she looked last night in that new sweater I gave her for Christmas. She walked me outside on her porch when it was time for me to go home, and it was real nice out there. There was this full moon, and the snow was all blue-white, like it gets in the moonlight, and the tree shadows were a deeper blue and real sharp, almost like someone took a brush and painted them there on the snow. It was quiet, too, and so cold that our breath came out like smoke. We stood there, just looking at it all for a while, and then Megan reached up and put her arms around my neck and kissed me. She smelled so good, kind of like sheets that have been hanging outside all day that your mom pulls in, throws on your head, and then says, "Sniff." Mmm. I could write about Megan forever. But I guess that won't help me get into college, will it? Okay, so what else is on my mind?

Well, there's the tri-meet coming up this Saturday. I'm really worried about that. There's a strong possibility that I'm going to get my butt kicked. Eastbrook High has a new heavyweight who supposedly looks like the Russian guy in *Rocky IV,* muscles and all. And I'm out of shape. I mean, I had the best intentions of working out during Christmas break, but . . . well, you know how that goes.

I don't suppose that's what colleges want to know either, though, huh? Mrs. Robinson says they usually want to know how you'd like to change the world or what the most significant event in your life was or something like that.

I don't really feel qualified to change the world, so I

guess maybe I'll go with the significant event. Let's see. What were some of the most significant events in my life so far? Well, getting my driver's license, for one. That was *the* most significant. You know what I mean? Freedom, man! Wheels! Let's be honest, what could be more significant to a seventeen-year-old guy? Unless . . . Get your mind out of the gutter, Carver. The essay's supposed to be based on a *true* incident, remember?

Okay, so how was getting my driver's license significant? I mean, everybody gets one, right? Well, almost everybody. But if you're not smart enough to get your driver's license, I doubt you'd be applying to college, so I guess colleges probably just assume that you've got your driver's license. Mrs. Robinson says significant stuff is supposed to teach you something, change you somehow. So . . . what did getting my license teach me?

Well, until I got my driver's license, I thought I was a pretty good driver. In fact, to tell you the truth, I thought I was probably about the best damn driver ever to come down the pike. Hey, that's a pun, isn't it? I bet colleges like puns. Anyway, not to brag, but I've been driving dirt bikes and quads since I was twelve, and I can handle just about any terrain New England can throw at me, so I figured a car on a road had to be cake, right? *Wrong.* Two days after I got my license, I got into an accident. And it was my fault! Well, not really. I hit this old lady in the rear—of her car, not her butt—but she stopped for a yellow light, in the rain! How stupid can you get? I mean, everybody knows the rule: light turns yellow, two more cars sneak through before it turns red, right? Well, not this old lady. So, anyhow, the law said it was my fault. The cop told me that in Massachusetts a car can jump the median into your lane, do a 180 right in front of you, and if you plow into it, you're still at fault. Which really stinks, because my sister, Kat, got rear-ended in New Hampshire a couple of years back, and it ended up being *her* fault. Talk about being in the wrong place at the wrong time, huh?

Anyway, as I was saying, I got into this accident, and I really *was* surprised because, like I said, I thought I'd be able to handle anything that came along in a car. I figured the accident must have been just a fluke or something. But then, six weeks later, I got into another accident! And it was my fault again! And this time, I guess it really was. I was at this intersection one night, see, and I had a red light, and this truck was coming up on the left. I thought it was a lane over, though I wasn't sure. ~~It's a little hard for me to judge stuff like that sometimes.~~ I suppose I should've waited till I *was* sure, but I was late for my curfew, as usual, so I decided to chance it. I started to turn right on red—and I plowed right into the side of the truck. There wasn't much I could say about that. I mean, it's hard to say someone hit the front of your car with the side of their truck.

My parents were UPSET.

"You know you can't take chances like that," my father said, then he launched into his you've-got-to-be-extra-careful speech.

It really bugs me when he gives me that speech. I get this tense feeling inside, and I feel like punching something. I don't want to be extra careful. I don't want to be *extra* anything. I just want to be regular—a regular kid, being regular careful, living a regular life. But I can't, because my parents are so uptight. They overreact to everything. Like when I got that speeding ticket for doing fifty in a thirty-five zone. I mean, c'mon. Does *anybody* actually drive thirty-five, other than my mother? My parents get *really* bent out of shape when I get speeding tickets. They ground me and take the car away and everything. They don't get *as* mad about accidents—mostly worried. Which is worse sometimes. After the truck accident, my mom actually had the nerve to say that maybe I shouldn't be driving at night.

Can you believe it? *Shouldn't be driving at night?* I'm seventeen years old, for Crissake. What am I supposed to do—have my friends chauffeur me around all the time, or my parents? Oh, they'd love that. I swear, that's what they really want—to keep me right under their thumbs, every minute.

"Or maybe we should get some truck mirrors mounted on the front of the car," my dad suggested.

"Oh yeah, that'd look real cool, Dad," I said. "A Buick Park Avenue with truck mirrors. Why don't we just get me a van, like all the other *handicapped* people?"

My dad's face kind of fell when I said that and I felt bad because I'd said it on purpose to blow his mind. My parents are such a pain. Always nagging, always pushing the panic button when the littlest thing goes wrong. And then, when I blow up, *they're* the ones who act all hurt and start saying stuff like they just love me and they're trying to look out for me and all the rest of the guilt junk parents are

7

so good at dumping on your head. And somehow, I'm the one who always ends up feeling lower than a snake's gut.

So I ended the discussion by pulling out my driver's license and waving it under their noses. "Look what it says on here," I told them. "It doesn't say, 'can't drive at night.' It doesn't say, 'can't drive without truck mirrors.' It just says, 'Driver's License.' Period. End of discussion. Okay?" I was kind of yelling by then. It seems like most of my discussions with my parents end up with me yelling.

So how did I get on that subject? Oh yeah, I was saying how getting my license taught me something. See, I finally had to admit to myself that maybe I *wasn't* the world's greatest driver. Not back then anyway. But that was several months ago. I'm a lot better now.

Still, I don't suppose that's the kind of significant stuff colleges are interested in either, huh? College isn't much about driving. It's more about reading and writing and stuff. I wonder why colleges are so big on writing? On my list of favorite things to do, writing's down pretty low, I gotta tell you. Not that I actually hate it. I mean, it's not as bad as Spanish or *calculus*. Now there's a subject that *really* sucks.

The funny thing about writing is, once you get into it, it's not that bad. Believe it or not, I had a poem published in a magazine a few years ago. I wrote it when I was fourteen. I still remember it by heart. It's called "The Falcon."

> *As the falcon sits*
> *on his lonely perch*
> *his heart is soaring*

through the deep blue sky.
He dreams of drifting
through the cool, crisp air
and seeing things to be.
The falcon sits
with his head sagging down
and his eyes staring up,
a chain around his leg.

Not bad, huh? My mom thought it was so good that, without my knowing it, she sent it in to a magazine. She was so excited when it got published. She started acting like I was going to grow up to be a poet or something. Give me a break. I mean, even if I wanted to, what kind of money do poets make? I've noticed that about life. The fun jobs don't pay much.

Where was I going with this anyway? Oh yeah, poetry. Well, I wouldn't want to be a poet, even if it paid big bucks. What I'd really like to be is a mechanic, one who specializes in dirt bikes, boat motors, snowmobiles–things like that. My parents would never go for it, though. They both went to college, and it's a really big deal to them that their kids go to college, too. Like Kat, my sister. She got into a great college, and my parents are *so* proud of her. I hope I can do as well. I don't know, though. Kat's a brain. But I'll try. I just hope that all this college stuff pays off, that when I'm there I can find some kind of career that I like, that isn't too hard, and that I can make a ton of money at. Then maybe someday, after I get rich, I can quit that career and do what I really want to do.

Anyway, back to my poem. Like I said, my mother got so excited about it being published that when we moved here last year, she brought it in and showed it to my new principal. And the principal got so excited that she asked me if they could publish it in the school newspaper, and, not wanting to get on the bad side of the new principal, I had to go along with it, right? Meanwhile, I'm ready to kill my mom because I can just picture what everybody is going to think of me when they hear that the new kid's a *poet*. I mean, think about it. Who in their right mind would do that to their kid? The funny thing is, though, it didn't turn out that bad. The kids actually thought the poem was cool, and they were even kind of impressed that it'd been published in a real magazine. Go figure, huh?

Actually, some poets *are* pretty cool. Like that guy Edgar Allan Poe. I wonder if he kept a journal? I bet it must have been pretty gruesome if he did. He wrote some creepy stuff.

"Quoth the Raven, 'Nevermore.'"

Cool.

You know who else was a cool poet? Robert Frost. I wish I could have hung around with him. Imagine taking a walk in the woods with Robert Frost. My favorite poem of his is "Birches." In fact, after I read it, I went out and tried swinging on a few. It's the coolest thing—just like he says in the poem. You climb way up to the very top, as far as you can go. And the tree puts up with you for just so long, then it s-l-o-w-l-y bends over and drops you real gently back on the ground again. Yeah.

The trouble with poems on the whole, though, is for

every good one, there's about a million lousy ones that don't make a lick of sense. And it's always the ones that make the least sense that English teachers assign for homework. I think they do it for spite. They assign these poems, see, and then they go home and crack open a beer and flop down on the couch and laugh their heads off just thinking about all their poor students staring at that poem and scratching their heads and trying to figure out what the hell the author was trying to say. It makes me mad just thinking about it. Stuff like that always makes me mad.

You know who's my favorite author of all? J. D. Salinger. He saw right through all that phoniness and stuff. When I read *Catcher in the Rye,* I thought, Man, this guy is talking about me. He knows just how I feel!

I hate phoniness, too. Like the English teachers and the lousy poems. Phony people make me so mad, I feel like punching them sometimes. But I don't. Not anymore anyway. I used to be quite a puncher when I was little. Kat was black and blue for a lot of years. But she deserved it back then. She grew up to be pretty cool, and we're good friends now, but when she was little, she had this mouth. She could cut me off at the knees and cut me off again and again. I never could think of anything fast enough and mean enough to say back to her, and even if I could have, she'd never let me get a word in edgewise. So I'd shut her up the only way I knew how—with my fist. Then she'd go blubbering to Mom and Dad—and guess who always ended up in trouble?

Whoever made up that "sticks and stones" stuff obviously didn't know my sister. Our parents never caught on either. I remember one time my kindergarten teacher called them into school because I was smushing kids' sandpiles and stomping on their block buildings. The teacher told my parents I needed an "outlet for my aggression," so they went out and bought me this big clown punching bag. Every day after school my mom would say, "Why don't you go down and punch your punching bag for a while, Luke?"

Well, that was fun about *once*. I mean, what kind of kick could anybody get out of punching a big plastic clown that keeps popping right back up and grinning at you? If they really wanted me to punch it, they should have put a tape recording of Kat's voice inside it.

Anyhow, I still *feel* like punching people sometimes, but I don't do it anymore. I guess that's maturing. I hope so anyway.

Man. Will you look at that? It's eleven o'clock already. Time flies when you're writing a journal, I guess. Wow, I wrote twelve pages, too. That oughta make Robinson happy. Good thing she's not going to read them.

Monday, January 6

Some people are so annoying. I can't believe how many kids kept up with their journals over vacation. One girl had half a notebook full! What a little kiss-butt. Robinson wasn't too happy when she saw I only had one entry. She wasn't even impressed that it was twelve pages long. She made me come and speak to her after class.

"One entry, Luke?" she said. "You had two full weeks off. That's fourteen days. And you only have one entry?"

"Well, it's a big one, though, Mrs. Robinson," I told her. "Twelve pages—that's a page a day if you don't count Christmas and New Year's."

She smiled then, so I figured she wasn't going to come down on me too hard. "Luke," she said, "the idea of a journal is to write a little bit every day, or almost every day. I'd much rather see twelve one-page entries than one twelve-page entry, okay?"

I shrugged. "I guess so," I said, "but I don't really see the difference. It still adds up to the same amount of writing if you ask me."

"It's not the amount of writing that matters, Luke," Mrs. Robinson explained, "it's the number of ideas you explore."

"Well, that's part of the problem," I told her. "I don't think I have that many ideas. Not that much has happened in my life."

Mrs. Robinson gave me a wry smile.

"Just write, Luke," she said. "I'm sure you'll discover

that your life has been more interesting than you think."

I shrugged again. "I'll do it," I said, "but I'm telling you, my life is pretty darn boring."

Mrs. Robinson arched one of her painted-on eyebrows.

"Are you trying to tell me," she said, "that nothing interesting or . . . different has ever happened to you?"

"Nothing significant enough to write about."

Mrs. Robinson straightened a pile of papers on her desk, then leaned back in her chair and looked up at me.

"Luke," she said, staring directly into my face, "I want you to take this assignment a little more seriously, okay? This is your junior year—*the* most important academic year for college-bound students, and I'm not seeing the effort from you that I'd like to see."

I looked at the floor.

"Has anything been . . . bothering you, Luke? Is there some reason you weren't able to keep up with your journal over the holidays?"

"No," I said. "I've just been . . . busy."

"I see." Mrs. Robinson nodded slowly, then let out a deep sigh. "Well, we're all busy, Luke," she said, "but part of growing up is learning to set priorities. This assignment should be a priority for you. You need the grade, and you need the writing practice. The college admissions process is even tougher now than it was a couple of years ago when your sister went through it. If you're hoping to get into the kind of school she got into, you've got to try harder."

I looked at her. "I'll try, Mrs. Robinson," I said.

She stared at me then in that funny way adults do when they're thinking about saying something but don't know if they should. I guess she decided she should, because she did.

"I would think that you of all people would have a lot to write about, Luke," she said.

~~I looked away, not that I was self conscious about her staring at me like that, but I was starting to get that tight feeling in my chest, the one I always get when people try to bring up my~~ I felt like telling her to mind her own business, but I figured she'd probably give me detention or something, so I didn't say anything.

After a long, awkward silence, Mrs. Robinson cleared her throat.

"I guess that will be all for now, Luke," she said, "I'll be checking the journals every day or two. I hope we won't have to have this conversation again."

"No ma'am," I said.

So there. I wrote three pages. That ought to make her happy.

Tuesday, January 7

*H*ere I am, at it again. I'm writing one page tonight, period. Doesn't Robinson realize I've got other classes besides hers? Who's got time to write in a stupid journal every night? And all so that I can go to four more years of school after high school. I wonder who came up with the idea of college anyway? Isn't twelve years of school enough torture to put a kid through?

Even Kat didn't like college much her first year. She was homesick a lot. She seems to like it now, though. I go up and visit her sometimes, and it's pretty cool. We go to parties and basketball games and stuff, and that's fun. The only thing is, the kids that are actually students there have to worry about studying and getting good grades.

Too bad. Imagine if they had colleges for fun stuff, like maybe dirt-bike riding. Or skiing, or boat racing! Man, I think I'm on to something here. I'd be a hero if I started a college like that. I can just hear the parents, though: "I'm not going to pay for any dirt-bike college. What kind of job are you going to get graduating from dirt-bike college?"

There's always a catch, isn't there?

I hope I can get into a college like Kat's. I've noticed that parents get a big kick out of bragging about where their kids go to college. Mine do anyway. They love bragging about Kat. Their faces light up whenever anybody asks them about her. Actually, come to think of it, their faces light up like that when they talk about any of their kids: Kat, Nick, and even *me*, only I don't know why.

Not that I've been a *bad* kid. I mean, I've known a lot worse, but I do tend to screw up a lot. When I read *Catcher in the Rye* I got kind of worried about myself, because you know how Holden Caulfield ends up in a mental institution? Well, I thought maybe I was crazy, too, because I hated phoniness the way he did, and because I screwed up a lot like he did. And then I heard that the guy who shot John Lennon was obsessed with *Catcher in the Rye,* and I started worrying that maybe I was going to grow up and shoot somebody or something. I've gotten over worrying about that, though. Like I said, I've learned how to keep those mad feelings inside. But I do seem to have more than my share of bad luck.

I can't seem to go more than six months without getting into some kind of trouble. I wonder if that's normal? I swear, the weirdest things happen to me. Like what I did to my dog, Daisy, a couple of weeks ago. Yellow Labs are the greatest, and Daisy's got to be the best dog in the world. Anyway, I chopped the end of her tail off. God, that was awful. I was chopping wood, and ~~she came up on my left side~~ all of a sudden there she was, like out of nowhere, and I didn't see her until it was too late. And the worst part was, she didn't even feel anything at first, so when I started shrieking and jumping around she thought it was a game or something and she started jumping, too, and wagging her tail all happy, and blood was splattering everywhere. I thought I was going to be sick. I really did. It was Christmas Eve, too.

She's okay now. We got her to the vet and got her fixed up. It sure ruined Christmas Eve, though. My whole family was upset. And of course my parents started in with the worrying again. Saying maybe I shouldn't be using an ax. Maybe I shouldn't be chopping wood. Jesus! When are they going to get it through their heads that I am seventeen years old?

"Did she come up on your left side?" my mother asked me. She asked it real timid, like *I* was the one who was hurt and she was afraid of hurting me more. I *hate* when she does that.

"It doesn't matter what side she came from!" I shouted. "She wasn't there. Then she was. That's all. It could have happened to anyone."

My parents gave each other that look then, like they share some kind of secret I don't know. God, I *really* hate it when they do that.

"Luke," my Dad said quietly. "Suppose it had been Nick who came up beside you in the woods, instead of Daisy?"

That took my breath away for a minute, imagining myself chopping off a piece of my little brother. But then, the more I thought about it, the madder I got.

"I think Nick's got brains enough not to sneak up behind somebody with an ax in his hand," I shouted. "Why don't you try to find something *stupider* to worry about!"

"You know you need to be extra careful, Luke."

Extra careful. Jeez! I get so tired of hearing that.

Whoa! I was only going to write one page, and I wrote four. I can't believe how fast time goes when I'm writing this stuff. But look what I've come up with. Another goose egg. I can just see a college admissions committee now: "Oh, here's an essay about a kid who chopped his dog's tail off. Just the type of student we're looking for. Send him an acceptance right away!" Jeez. I'm hopeless.

Wednesday, January 8

Man, this is getting to be a drag—sitting in this same chair every night, staring at the same annoying little rip in the wallpaper. Strange how your eye is always drawn to the ugly stuff, isn't it? I mean, here's a whole wall full of nice, pretty wallpaper, and what do I keep focusing on? One ugly little ripped piece. ~~I feel like people look at me that way sometimes, like it doesn't matter how cool I'm dressed, or how great my hair looks or anything, because when they look at me all they seem to focus on is my~~

This wallpaper is getting on my nerves, but then, so is everything else lately. I've even started chewing my fingernails again, and I haven't done that since—when? Eighth grade? But I had a good reason to be stressed out then.

I guess I must be worried about the tri-meet. Or maybe it's Megan. She said something today that kind of bugged me. She was talking about the junior prom—which is still *months* away—and she was talking like it was an absolute *given* that we'd be going together. Like we were already "a couple." Why do girls do that? You go out five or six times, and suddenly they're thinking about forever. I mean, I like her and all, but I'm not ready for forever. I didn't even really want to buy her a Christmas present, but she just assumed I was and kept dropping hints about what she was getting me until I was kind of forced into it. I tried not to get her anything too personal. I mean, a sweater isn't any big deal, is it? She actually looked kind of disappointed when she opened it, like maybe she was hoping for jewelry or something. I stay away from jewelry. Girls seem to think it signals some kind of commitment even if it's nothing but earrings. Jewelry has a very committing effect on girls.

I was committed once. To a girl, I mean, not to a mental institution, although that's kind of weird when you think about it. It's the same word, isn't it? I wonder if that means anything? Anyhow, I'm not really sure how I got committed to this girl. I was pretty young, thirteen or fourteen. She was real cute: part Hawaiian, small, with a nice figure and the longest, blackest hair you've ever seen. She was nice, too. We "went out" a few times, which back then meant my parents drove us to the movies or the mall, and then somehow, she started telling me how mean her parents were and stuff, and I started feeling bad for her. Then the next thing I knew, she was telling me she loved me and that I had changed her whole life and made her happy and everything. I mean, I didn't do that much, just the movies, like I said, and I hung out with her in school a little bit, but it seemed to make such a big difference to her. And then she asked me if I loved her back, and I didn't want to hurt her feelings or anything, you know? My mother always told me to think about other people's feelings. So I guess I said yes.

Well, that was all she had to hear. She started talking about *forever* in a big way. I mean, house, kids, everything! And she wasn't just talking about it to me. She was telling the whole school! It was getting very awkward, and then she started expecting me to spend all my time with her.

But the thing was, I really did like her, and I didn't want to break her heart or anything, so I just kept going along with it all. I don't know where it would have ended up if my father hadn't gotten fired.

That was just pure luck. Not that it was the best thing that ever happened. I mean, my family wasn't too thrilled. I wasn't either, actually, because he ended up finding a job at the other end of the state, and we had to move, and I had to leave all my friends and my school. But it was helpful in that it really cooled off the romance. It was still pretty hard, though. She thought we were going to wait for each other and all that, and she wrote me just about every day, and when I didn't write back she kept calling me up and complaining and having her friends call. After about six months, I was so sick of it all that one night I just flat out told her it was over. And that was pretty awful. She really cried, and I hate to hurt anybody like that. I know girls think guys are cold and mean and have no feelings or anything, but that's not true, not with me anyway. I felt bad for a long time. ~~Especially since she stuck by me through all the surgery and everything. A lot of my other friends kind of disappeared after a while.~~ Anyhow, that's why I'm so careful about girls now. I don't want to get in a situation like that again, not until I'm ready to get married, which is a long way off.

The crummy part is, I really like Megan a lot and I want to keep going out with her, but I'm going to have to stop it now before she gets too serious. I couldn't take breaking *her* heart. I really couldn't.

I wonder if that's normal? I seem to worry a lot about

whether I'm normal or not. For example, I don't seem to be able to think of girls the way a lot of guys do. Like sex objects. I mean, I *do* think of them as sex objects, of course, but I also can't help thinking of them as people. Maybe it's because Kat and I have turned out to be such good friends and she makes me think about how girls feel.

The hard thing is, so many of the guys I know seem to think that girls are just bodies with no heads or hearts. All they care about is how many they can get, and they don't care what they have to say or do to get them. It makes me mad to think guys might be phony like that with my sister. Tell her lies and stuff, you know? Kat's pretty cool, though. I think she could see through those kinds of guys. I hope so anyway.

Anyhow, what I'm getting at is that guys brag a lot about what they've done with girls. And that's when it gets hardest, because I don't want my friends to think I'm a wimp or anything. So sometimes I make stuff up, but I feel bad about that, too, because it's phony, you know? And by going along with them, I'm sort of encouraging the whole business.

But then I think, What if we're all lying? What if a lot of guys feel the way I do, but nobody will admit it because nobody wants everyone else to think they're a wimp? Then I think, Maybe I should just come out and tell the truth, and then all those other guys would be so relieved, they'd all start telling the truth, and we could get rid of the phoniness once and for all. And I think, Maybe I'll say something. Not in the middle of the locker room or anything, but when there's just a few of us hanging out. But then I get this mental picture of all of them staring at me like I'm gay or something.

So I just keep lying. I guess maybe I am a wimp.

Hey, four pages again. What do you know? I'm getting to be a regular Ernest Hemingway.

Thursday, January 9

I think I need a change of scenery. Either that, or I'm going to grab that little piece of freakin' wallpaper I've been staring at for the last hour and yank it off the wall. I'm tired. I was up late last night reading history and studying for a math quiz, which I think I failed anyway. Man, life sucks sometimes. But . . . hey . . . not all the time. It just started snowing! Like gangbusters! Hey, maybe school will be canceled tomorrow. Man, I hope so.

That has got to be the best feeling in the world–when you go to bed and it's snowing, and you wake up in the middle of the night, and everything is sort of extra quiet, and you look out your window and you can see by the streetlight that it's *still* snowing. . . . And you say a little prayer, even though you know God probably has more important things to worry about than school cancellations. But maybe not, though, because He made kids, you know? He knows how they are, so maybe He just likes to be nice every now and then and take time out from the real heavy-duty prayer stuff to answer a little prayer that will make kids happy. I'd do that if I were God. I really would.

Anyhow, you say this little prayer and you climb back into bed, and your bed feels extra soft and warm just because you know it's snowing outside, and you kind of drift back to sleep with this hopeful feeling inside and a little smile on your face. And then your dad sticks his head in the door and says, "Stay in bed. No school today."

Yes! That is the *best* feeling in the world!

So, of course, I get up immediately. Why is that, I wonder? I mean, every other day when my alarm goes off, my eyelids feel like they weigh about ten pounds each, and my body aches and moans and groans and begs for one more minute, one more lousy minute. And I lie there forcing my eyelids open a little at a time, catching glimpses of the clock, putting off getting up until my mom is yelling and the bus is practically at the door. Then I have to jump up and rush around like a maniac, and all the while my body is begging me to crawl back into that bed for just one . . . more . . . nice . . . long . . . sweet . . . minute. And sometimes I give in and lie back down, which is the greatest torture of all, because my body just sinks into the mattress and sighs this long, "Ahhhhhhhhh. . . ." And then my mom yells, and I have to rip my poor old bod right back out into the cold again.

But on a snow day, when I could stay in bed as long as I want, my eyes pop open and my body jumps up, feeling like it could run the Boston Marathon. Ironic, isn't it?

Actually, it's pretty interesting when you think about it. Maybe I should write my college essay on that, on how your mind can control your body and stuff. Like those Hindu guys who can walk through fire and sleep on nails. I think there's a lot to that spiritual stuff.

My mom and dad took me to a spiritual healing service once, back in eighth grade when I was having all the operations. They heard about this priest who was famous for holding these healing services, and I guess they figured we needed all the help we could get, so they asked me about it. I thought it was a really stupid idea, but I could see they had their hearts set on it. At least my dad did, and I figured what did we have to lose, so we went.

Let me tell you, it was pretty freaky. Most of the people who were there must have been to these things before and knew what to expect, because they didn't seem too surprised or anything, but my parents and me . . . well, we almost walked out a couple of times. We ended up staying, though. I'm still not sure why.

At first it didn't seem *too* strange. I mean, the church was pretty normal looking, and the priest seemed to be an okay guy. He started out just talking about Jesus and other stuff you'd expect, and there was the usual singing and praying. But then, after about fifteen minutes, the priest shouted something and pointed at the audience. Next thing we knew, all these people jumped up and started waving their hands back at him and talking all at once as loud as they could. The really freaky thing, though, was that they weren't speaking English. In fact, they weren't speaking anything I'd ever heard before. They were all talking in different languages and making weird sounds, some of them even like animals.

"What the heck are they doing?" I whispered to my dad.

He looked pretty startled, too. "I think they call it 'speaking in tongues,'" he whispered back.

I was about ready to bolt when I heard that, I can tell you, and I could tell by the look on my mom's face that she was about ready to run, too, but my dad hadn't had enough just yet.

"Take it easy," he told me. "Let's see what happens next."

"Dad . . . ," I said.

He turned to look at me then, and I could see that he was really nervous. That's when it hit me how much he had his hopes up.

"Dad," I said quietly. "You . . . you're not really . . . expecting to see a miracle or anything, are you?"

He glanced at my mother, then looked back at me. His Adam's apple bobbed, and for a second his eyes got kind of shiny.

"Let's . . . just see what happens next, okay?" he said. I looked at my mom and saw the plea in her eyes: *Let him believe just a little longer.* I think maybe a part of her wanted to believe, too.

"All right," I told my dad. "We'll see what happens next."

Well, what happened next was that the whole noise thing died down and people started getting up and getting in line.

"See, I told you," said my dad. "They're lining up for the blessing. It's just about over. Come on, I'll walk up there with you."

He got up and almost dragged me into the line. I looked back at my mom, and she gave me this little smile that was supposed to be reassuring, I guess, but she didn't look any too sure herself.

"I don't think I like this, Dad," I whispered. "Can't we just watch?"

"Shush," Dad whispered back. "There's nothing to worry about. It's just a blessing. You've had blessings before."

Okay, I decided. He's right. I've had blessings before. The priest touches your head or makes the sign of the cross on your forehead, mumbles a few words, and you're done. Right?

Wrong.

The line starts to move forward, see, and I'm just kind of shuffling along, waiting my turn, when all of a sudden I notice these bodies lying on the floor up ahead. My heart went *boing!* I mean, I'm talking *bodies* sprawled out on the floor! So I start paying attention to what's going on up at the front of this line, and I see the priest give this guy a blessing, and the next thing you know, the guy faints, and these people behind him catch him and drag him over with the rest of the bodies.

Whoa! That was it. Time out. This boy had seen enough. I tapped my father on the back.

"Hey!" I whispered. "I'm outta here."

My dad turned around. He was looking a little pale himself. He looked behind me and then around at the people sitting in their seats. His Adam's apple bobbed a couple more times. I think he wanted to bolt, too, but he didn't want to make a scene. My dad's very concerned about making scenes, especially in church. The nuns drilled that into him when he was a kid, I guess. He kept looking backward and forward, and meanwhile, the people ahead of us are dropping like flies and we're getting closer and closer to the front.

"Dad!" I whispered. "Let's get outta here, *now!*"

Dad shook his head. "We can't."

"What!"

"Shush." He looked around again. "We can't. It's too late."

"Too late!" By this time, my heart was whamming off the walls of my chest like a squash ball. I thought of just making a break for it and leaving my dad standing there, but he was giving me this look, begging me with his eyes. I knew then that I was going to have to go through with it. When my dad gives me that look, I'm pretty well stuck.

There were only a couple more people ahead of us by then, and I was relieved to see that some of the people who had passed out earlier were starting to wake up. A few of them had gotten to their feet and had gone back to their seats already.

"I don't care what anybody says, I'm *not* passing out!" I whispered fiercely into my father's ear.

He threw an amused glance back at me. "You don't *have* to pass out," he answered, then he stepped to one side, and it was my turn.

"Come forward, son," said the priest. He held his arms out to me. My face started to burn and my head got heavy, as if all the blood in my body had rushed up there and gotten clogged and couldn't get down again. I struggled to stay calm, stepping forward like the priest had asked. Two people closed in behind me, the ones who were supposed to catch me, I guess, when I fell. Only I *wasn't* going to fall.

"What is it you've come to ask, my son?" said the priest.

I looked into his eyes. He had strange eyes–kind of hypnotic. Like once you looked at them, it was hard to look away. Then I found myself saying something I didn't plan on saying.

"I . . . I came to be healed," I said.

The priest gave me a sad smile. "There are many kinds of healing, my son," he said gently. "Let us pray together for God's mercy and the faith to accept His kind of healing."

The priest put his hand on my head, and then the two people behind me moved in close and started rubbing my back, and they all began to pray. Then the strangest thing happened. I began to feel warm all over, warm and very weak. My legs started to feel like jelly, and I knew that I could faint if I wanted to. But I didn't want to, so I fought. I concentrated as hard as I could on standing, just standing until the prayer was through. It seemed like a long time, but at last the people moved away, and the priest put his arms around me and hugged me. "Bless you, my son," he whispered, then he let me go.

I was shaking all over from weakness, but I still wouldn't fall. My dad came over and took my arm, and then someone took my other arm, and with their help I was able to walk, but my legs felt so trembly. At last I reached my seat and practically fell into it. My mom was staring at me, like she couldn't believe what she was seeing. I didn't blame her. I couldn't believe what I was feeling. I didn't know what it was, but it was powerful all right.

Then, after I'd sat there a while, I covered my right eye and looked around. Nothing had changed. Nothing. Not that I'd expected it would, but for some reason I started to cry then, right there in the middle of the whole church. It was just a couple of tears at first, and I tried real hard to hold back, but then it was like a flood, and there was nothing I could do to stop it. I put my head down in my hands and sobbed and sobbed all through the rest of the service, cried until there wasn't a tear left in me to cry.

My parents didn't say anything. They just rubbed my back and let me cry. Later, in the car on the way home, they asked me if I was okay.

I looked up and saw my dad's eyes in the rearview mirror. They looked like a tired old man's eyes with all those little worry lines at the corners. When had he gotten so old, I wondered.

"Yes," I said quietly, "I'm fine." Then I closed my eyes and leaned my head back against the seat. I was tired, too. So, so tired . . .

Just like I am now.

Friday, January 10

I can't believe it, but I think this writing stuff is getting to be a habit. When I woke up this morning and saw how beautiful everything was outside, I actually found myself thinking about how I could describe it in my journal.

I finally decided the snow was sad. I know that sounds dumb, but that's how I feel sometimes, sad because something is so beautiful. I feel that way a lot, like in the summer, on Cape Cod, when the sunset spreads across the water like spilled paint and the sailboats stand out against it like cut-paper silhouettes; or here at home, when fall comes to the mountain and the colors of the season make the maples in my backyard look like they're on fire. I don't know why that makes me feel sad. ~~Maybe because I can't remember anymore how it used to look.~~

We must have had a little freezing rain last night before the snow started, because the snow stuck to everything—every blade of grass, every little branch and twig of every tree. When I woke up, the mountains looked like some giant had shaken down a great big can of baby powder all over everything. Then the sun came over the ridge, and the snow turned from gray to pink to gold, then so dazzling white that it hurt to look at it. I wanted so much to save it that I went out and took a bunch of pictures, knowing all along that it was no use. Pictures are never the same as the real thing.

It was too pretty a day to stay inside. Megan came over, and we went for a walk up along the ridge. You can see for miles up there. We call it Top-o'-the-World, because that's just what it feels like up there. It's the best place to camp—so close to the stars, with the lights of the valley twinkling down below. Lots of times when I'm camping up there with my friends, I get up real early, before anyone else, and I go sit on the very edge, absolutely quiet, and watch the morning come. Indians used to live all around here, and when I'm sitting on the mountain like that, all by myself, I wonder if some Indian guy used to sit there and watch the morning come, too. And I know he did, and I feel connected to him somehow, peaceful.

I didn't feel that way today, though; I had a lot of stuff on my mind. I just find myself thinking a lot since I started this journal. I'm not sure it's good. I mean, there's a lot of stuff I don't like thinking about, and I've spent a lot of years learning how to not think about it, and now here I am thinking about it again. I don't think it's fair that teachers can make you do stuff that you don't want to do like that.

Anyhow, I guess I wasn't talking much up on the mountain today. But that didn't seem to bother Megan. When everything is that beautiful, talk seems kind of cheesy anyway. I mean, like, what can you say? "Isn't this beautiful?" Doesn't quite fit the bill, does it? There should be some better words for things like that.

You know what *was* beautiful, though? Megan. She had this blue-green parka on, with a hood with white fuzz all around. And with everything so white, her eyes looked bluer than the sky, and her cheeks and lips were rosy from the cold, and little wisps of red hair poked out from under her hood and fluttered around in the wind. God, she was beautiful. I really wanted to kiss her, but I didn't. I think she was disappointed that I didn't, but she didn't make a big deal about it. That's what makes it so hard. She's so darn nice. I mean, I can handle it when a girl is beautiful and obnoxious, or if she's nice but kind of unattractive. I'm okay then. But Megan—she's got to go and be beautiful and nice, too. It really isn't fair.

I mean, she was content just to be with me, without talking or anything. It's like she understood about words not being good enough. She was happy just to walk along and look at everything. How many girls would do that? I mean, usually they chatter a mile a minute, and you have the hardest time thinking what to say back to them. And you start to get nervous, because they're talking so much and you're hardly saying anything, and you think they must think you're a real dork with no personality or something. So you try even harder to think of something to talk about, and you can't think of a thing, so you keep laughing like a goof and saying really lame things like, "no kidding," "uh-huh," and "no way." And you feel like such a dork. I hate it when girls make you feel like a dork.

The funny thing is, I can be friends with girls, and then I can talk just fine. But as soon as it's a date or something, everything changes. Except with Megan. Maybe that's because she and I are interested in a lot of the same things, and when she talks it's really easy to talk back. She's not phony either. Like the other day. We were studying up in my room, and she saw this stack of old records sitting next to my stereo.

"What are you doing with these?" she asked.

I was working on a calculus problem, and I almost had the answer, so I wasn't paying real close attention.

"Making a mix tape," I said.

"Oh yeah? What kind?"

"Just some oldies that I don't have on disc."

"Cool."

She started looking through the pile, and I went back to my problem. Then I heard a little giggle.

"John Denver?" she said.

"What?" I looked up and saw her holding up one of my parents' John Denver records. Now, if she were some other girl, I probably would've turned red and made up some lie about how I didn't know that record was in there or something, because liking John Denver isn't all that cool, you know? I mean it's fine if you're forty, but it's kind of corny when you're seventeen. But with Megan, somehow I knew I could be myself.

"Yeah," I said.

"You really like John Denver?" she asked.

I hesitated a minute, then said, "Yeah, what about it?"

"Nothing," she said. "I just can't believe you like him, too."

"Too?" I said.

"Yeah." She nodded. "I think he's great. I felt really bad when he died."

"Yeah, me too," I said quietly.

Then she came over and bounced down on the bed. "Which John Denver song is your favorite?" she asked.

I debated a minute or two about telling her, but then I

figured, What the heck? "'Grandma's Feather Bed,'" I said.

"No way!" Megan shrieked, and jumped up. "Mine, too." She held out the record. "Let's play it."

So we played it, and we sang along at the top of our lungs, goofing around like we were playing fiddles and stuff. And when it was over, we just fell down on the bed and laughed and laughed. It sounds really corny when I say it now, but it was fun.

"When my sister and brother and I were little," I told her, "my dad and mom used to pick us up and dance us all around the room to that song."

Megan smiled. "That's cool," she said. "No wonder you like it so much."

That's what I mean about her. She understands stuff like that.

"There's another one I like, too," I told her. "'Wildflowers in a Mason Jar.'"

"I don't know that one," she said.

"It's great. I'll play it for you."

I put it on, and we both sat down and listened. Megan's eyes got kind of soft and dreamy. Not that it's a romantic song or anything—it's about a kid and his grandfather. But it's one of those songs that make you think and remember things. Maybe even things you never realized before. When it ended, she put her hand over mine and squeezed.

"You're a real special guy, you know that, Luke?" she said.

I looked away. Not that I was self-conscious or anything, but when she said that, it made my heart beat real fast, and I knew that if I kept looking at her, I'd kiss her. And I'm starting to worry about the way I feel when I kiss her.

Like today, up there on the ridge. If I had held her there, in the middle of all that baby-powder snow, and kissed her like I wanted to, I'm not sure I'd have ever wanted to let her go again, and *that* scares the hell out of me.

Saturday, January 11

I got my butt handed to me at the meet today—handed to me on a platter, man! Is that *significant,* I wonder. Jeez. I'm not talking a nice, "Here is your butt. Would you kindly remove it from the ring" type of platter. I'm talking, "Here is your sorry little wuss of an ass, man! Drag it *outta* here!"

The guy teched me out, teched me out fifteen to zero! What a wuss I am. And then, as if that wasn't bad enough, in the second match, I'm wrestling this big, Pillsbury doughboy of a kid. You know the kind: huge but soft as a grape? Anyway, I can see I may not get a pin because he outweighs me by at least fifty pounds and I can barely get my arms around him, but I'm teching him like crazy, and I figure, Well, it won't make up for the humiliation in the first match, but at least I'm redeeming myself a little. And *then!*—I still can't believe it—the third period started, and Doughboy chose the down position. As soon as the buzzer sounded, I grabbed him around the chest, but he got his feet under him and stood up. I still had my arms around him, so I arched my back and tried to flip him over my leg. Only I slipped, because this guy was sweating buckets all over the mat. The next thing I know, I'm on my back, and Doughboy lands on top of me and knocks the wind out of me! Well, that did it. I was dead. All he did was roll over on me, and he got the pin. Pinned! By a doughboy! I still can't believe it.

By the third match, I was a nervous wreck. I won, but only by a couple of points, which was a disgrace in itself—

their first-string heavyweight was out with an injury, and I was wrestling the second-string kid. I should have killed him by a mile.

I hate wrestling. I don't know why I do it. The practices are hell, way worse than football. And I ought to know, because I play them both. You practice all week till you practically retch your brains out (and sometimes you do), then you go to the meets and you sit there waiting your turn and all you can think of is, Why am I here? I could be home, watching TV, riding my dirt bike, shooting a few hoops. . . . I mean, nobody is *making* me do this. I can leave if I want to. But for some ungodly reason, you always stay.

I don't know. Maybe it wouldn't be so bad if I weren't the heavyweight. The little guys get to go first, and then they can relax. But not me. I've got to sit through the whole meet, staring across the mat at the other guy, who's almost always bigger than me—I'm 220, and the weight class goes up to 275. So I check him out and try to psych myself up, try to tell myself I'm fast and I'm tough and I know more moves . . . all that bull. I look up at the stands, at my parents and my buddies who came to cheer me on, and then at my teammates, all counting on me, especially when the matches are close (and they *always* are). And then I look at Megan, and my heart starts racing about a million miles an hour, and the next thing I know, I have to run out and go to the bathroom. Then I come back in, sit back down, stare across the mat at the guy I have to wrestle—and it starts all over again. Finally, it's time to warm up, so I run out to the bathroom one last time. And when I come back in, I look across the mat, and the guy I have to wrestle has taken off his warm-ups. I get a look at all the muscles he's been hiding, and this pit forms in my stomach. So I start talking to myself, trying to tell myself he's not so tough, I can take him, and I feel like running to the bathroom again, but there isn't time. So I take off my warm-ups, put on my headgear and face mask, and pace around, taking deep breaths until they call me out on the mat.

Those are the times I wish I still had Coach Vanetti. He was my coach at my old school. I can still remember the day I told him I wanted to go out for the team. He must've thought I was nuts. I was nothing but a big old marshmallow then, so soft from not being able to play sports for such a long time.

"You sure you want to wrestle?" he asked me.

"Yeah," I said.

"You don't want to try something a little less intense? You're tall. How about basketball?"

"No," I said. "I want to wrestle."

He nodded his head and looked me over good. "You're a big guy for fourteen," he said.

I nodded.

"You'll have to be a heavyweight."

"I know."

"But you're a small heavyweight. It won't be easy."

"I know."

Coach Vanetti nodded thoughtfully. "Wrestling's a dangerous sport, son," he said. "Don't you think it's a big risk for someone like you?"

I didn't answer.

"What does your doctor think?" he asked.

"He says it's up to me. I just have to wear sports glasses," I said.

Coach Vanetti frowned. "You can't wear glasses wrestling, son," he said. "They'll get ripped right off your face."

I didn't budge. "I want to wrestle," I said again. "It's real important to me."

Coach nodded. "Well then," he said, "we'll find a way." He stuck out his hand. "Welcome to the team."

Then he got on my back and rode me like a drill sergeant. No sympathy, no special treatment. Anytime he thought I was slacking off, he'd get right up in my face and scream and swear and make me work twice as hard. It felt good to be treated like that, like everyone else. In fact, it felt great.

Coach Vanetti was the one who came up with the mask. He went through all the sports catalogs until he found this weird padded thing for people with broken noses. It snaps to your headgear, and when I put my glasses on under it, no one can rip them off. It took some getting used to because it cuts way down on visibility, ~~and mine was cut down already~~. I've gotten so I like that, though. Helps me focus. I'm not sure I could wrestle without it now; it'd be scary, I think. ~~Not just because I might get hurt, but because~~ I'd feel so . . . naked. Besides, it's gotten to be my trademark. Everyone knows "the guy with the mask."

I lost a lot of matches that first year, but Coach Vanetti always made me feel like I'd won somehow, or at least like

I'd win for sure the next time. There's this thing—call it "the winning spirit" if you want. But it's real. Anybody who plays a sport can tell you. When you've got it, you can't lose; and when you don't have it, you can't win. And sometimes it's there, right with you, and you can feel it, but then it starts to slip away, and you reach for it and claw at it, but it slips right through your fingers and there's nothing you can do but watch it go. But there are a few people out there who know how to grab it and pull it back. Coach Vanetti was one of those people. By the end of the season, I was winning every match. I could be down to my last ounce of strength, but then I'd look over at Coach, and somehow he'd make me reach way down inside myself and find a little more. He was all excited about my future. He had these really great plans for me. And then we moved.

I think getting a new coach must be kind of like getting a new father. It takes a while to let him into your life, and he can't ever take the place of the old one. My new coach is a real nice guy and all, but he isn't Coach Vanetti. I knew right after the first practice that if I was going to win from that point on, I was going to have to do it on my own. But I did okay. I won a couple of matches, and then the next thing I knew, word got around and everybody in the whole school was coming out to see me wrestle.

In fact, there was this one meet pretty early on that I'll never forget. The score was close going into my match, and the kid I had to wrestle was pretty much the same size I was. He was good, too. He'd placed real high in the state finals the year before. And he had an attitude. You know the kind. Acted like he didn't even want to be there, like I wasn't good enough for him to bother with. Well, we went out and we started, and unfortunately he *was* really good. For a while there, I thought he was going to prove his point good and quick, but then I settled down and forgot about my friends and my teammates—forgot about everything but the match. I started planning ahead instead of just reacting, and the score began evening up. We went back and forth, back and forth. He'd get a couple of points, I'd get a couple. Back and forth. By the end of the second period, the whole gym was going nuts because I guess nobody in our league had ever lasted past the first round with this guy before.

So, anyhow, the third period was about to start, and it was his choice. He chose the neutral position, probably because he figured he could take me down. Anyhow, the whistle blew and we started circling. Then all of a sudden, I heard this voice boom out of the stands. I recognized it right away. It was my new friend, Hutch.

"Car-ver!" he shouted in this funny, deep Bluto voice he uses sometimes. And as soon as he yelled it, a bunch of the other guys picked up on it and started stomping their feet and yelling it, too, all in that same Bluto voice. "Car-ver, Car-ver!"

For some reason, that really got the old adrenaline pumping through my veins. I shot in and grabbed the guy's leg. Down he went—two points for me! A huge roar went up from the crowd, and the whole gym started stomping and chanting, "Car-ver, Car-ver!" All these kids who'd only just met me, who hardly knew me from a hole in the wall, were shouting my name! They were loving me. Loving me because I could wrestle.

I don't remember exactly what happened after that. I just know I suddenly felt unbeatable again. A minute later, the kid was on his back and the ref was on his knees, face to the mat. Then I heard the slap of the ref's hand, followed by the whistle—that sweet, sweet whistle—and I jumped to my feet. The ref raised my arm in the air, and everyone was clapping and shouting and whistling. . . .

And that's why I wrestle. And it's my own damn fault I lost today. I was getting cocky. I let myself get out of shape. I let everybody down, especially the team, and after they went and made me captain this year, too. And me only a junior. That was a real honor, and I'm not living up to it. So God spanked me. He has a way of doing that. But this time, I deserved it. I'm going to Coach on Monday, tell him I'm soft, tell him he's gotta toughen up on me.

And another thing—I've made up my mind. I've got to break up with Megan. She's just getting too distracting. Like today. She came to the meet a little late, and there were no seats left, so she sat on Tony Lieberman's lap. Now, I know they're just friends and all, and I know she didn't mean anything by it, but it was very distracting just the same. I mean, how am I supposed to concentrate when my girl is sitting on Tony Lieberman's lap? It might not have been so bad if she were sitting on some little dork's lap, but Tony Lieberman is a good-looking guy. It really was *very* distracting. I have an awful lot of stuff on my mind right now anyway. I just don't have time for a girlfriend.

Monday, January 13

Mrs. Robinson was pretty happy when she checked my journal today. I have fifty pages! I think that's more than I've written in my whole life.

"That's very impressive, Luke," she said.

"Yeah," I told her, "and I did it myself, too. It's all my handwriting. See?"

She grinned. "I believe you, Luke," she said. "And to be honest, I'm not as surprised as you seem to be. I've always been impressed with the way you can write—when you put your mind to it."

"Really?" I said.

She nodded.

"I had a poem published once," I told her.

"I know," she said with a smile.

I smiled, too, then looked down at my journal and sighed. "I don't seem to be coming up with a lot of essay ideas, though," I said.

"Don't worry about the essay ideas yet," she said. "Just have fun exploring your thoughts."

Fun, huh? I'm not sure I'd go as far as to call it fun. I have to admit that I'm not hating it anymore, though. In fact, I find myself *wanting* to write about stuff more and more—especially when I'm mad, like I am right now, at my mother.

I was sitting in the family room when she got home today, just about to start my writing. I was feeling pretty good about it, too, after all the nice stuff Mrs. Robinson said. But my mother can turn a good mood sour faster than lemon juice can curdle milk.

"What are you doing home already?" she asked. "Did you get out of practice early?"

"Yeah."

"Why?"

"I don't know. Coach had to go somewhere."

My mother nodded and looked at my journal. "What are you writing?" she asked.

"Nothing."

"Is it something for school?"

"Yeah."

"A paper or something?"

"Yeah."

"Really? What about?"

"Nothing."

She frowned then. "Why are you so noncommunicative lately, Luke?" she asked.

Noncommunicative. Don't you love these words parents come up with? "I'm not *noncommunicative*," I said. "I'm just busy, okay? I've got wrestling. I've got school. I've got you guys on my back about my grades. . . ."

My mother stared at my hands. "When did you start biting your nails again?" she asked.

I rolled my eyes.

"Is something bothering you, Luke?" she asked.

"Yes," I snapped. "*You are.* Would you just leave me alone? I've got a ton of writing to do."

"Well, what's the assignment?" she asked. "Maybe I can help."

"No, you can't."

"How do you know if–"

"All right," I said sharply. "Fine. We've got to write these essays in English in a few weeks about something significant that happened in our lives. And we're keeping journals to help us come up with ideas. Okay? Any suggestions?"

My mother looked at me strangely. "Well, why don't you write about–"

"No!" I snapped.

My mother turned her hands palm up in a gesture of frustration. "Luke," she said. "You didn't even let me finish my sentence. How do you know what I was going to say?"

"I just know, okay?"

I stared at her and she stared back. I could see the old familiar worry creeping into her eyes, and it irritated me. I didn't have the time or patience to deal with that stuff just then.

"I just thought–," she began.

"I know what you thought," I interrupted, "and I don't care, okay?"

She bit her lip. "All right," she said quietly. "As long as you're sure you're okay."

"Yes." I rubbed my eyes tiredly. "I'm okay. I just don't want any advice, all right? You don't know how I feel. Just because something seems significant to you doesn't mean it's significant to me."

My mother didn't look like she believed me, but she shrugged her shoulders at last and turned away. "All right," she said quietly.

• • •

What is it with people, I wonder? Why does everybody keep dwelling on stuff that happened years ago? Why can't they forget it, like I have? What happened, happened, okay? I don't want to dredge up ancient history. I'd rather write about something else. Anything else. Like . . . I don't know . . . how about . . . birds? Yeah. I'd much rather write about birds. Look at all those birds out there at my mom's feeder. I wonder how birds like living outside all winter? It's really cold out today. Not much above zero, and with the windchill up here on the mountain, it's probably thirty below. I wonder why they don't freeze? I mean, look at their skinny little feet!

I saw on the news where some guy froze to death climbing Mount Washington up in New Hampshire a couple of weeks ago. The windchill was eighty below. I wonder what would make somebody climb Mount Washington when the windchill is eighty below? I think I'm pretty adventurous, a lot more than most people, but even I wouldn't do that. I mean, not at eighty below.

I'd climb Mount Washington, though. I'd love to climb Mount Washington. I climbed the face of Top-o'-the-World one day with Hutch back in the fall. We'd ridden up there on our bikes, and we were just kind of standing up there, looking at the view, when Hutch looked over the edge.

"Hey," he said, "it'd be pretty cool to climb down there, huh?"

I looked down, too. To tell you the truth, I'd never thought too much about climbing down before that, because it's pretty steep, you know? I mean, it's the kind of thing that when you stand by the edge and look down, your legs start quivering. Mine don't anymore because I'm used to it, but when people first go up there, their legs always quiver. My mom still stands about ten feet back from the edge every time she goes up there and keeps yelling at us, "Come back here now. You're making me nervous." Like I said, everything makes her nervous.

Anyway, when I looked down this time, I noticed that it wasn't really a sheer cliff. There were little jags in the rock all the way down, just perfect for putting your feet on. I started getting excited just thinking about making a climb like that.

"Wanna do it?" I asked Hutch.

Hutch looked a little surprised, like maybe he'd been asking a rhetorical question, one of those just-kind-of-thinking-out-loud kinds. Anyhow, he thought a little longer, and then he said, "Maybe we better not, Luke. You . . . uh, you know how your mom worries."

I looked at him. "My mom?" I said. "What has my mom got to do with anything?"

"Well"–Hutch swallowed–"she kind of . . . made me promise to look out for you."

"SHE WHAT?" I could feel the muscles in my jaw bulging out as I stared at him in disbelief.

Hutch pushed a hand nervously through his hair. "She . . . worries about you, Luke," he said. "She asked me not to let you do anything dumb."

I clenched my teeth and sucked a big breath of air in through my nose.

"So," I said through my clenched teeth. "Now my mother thinks I need a baby-sitter?"

"C'mon, Luke. Lighten up," said Hutch. "You have to admit, you've done some dumb things in the past."

"Oh, and you haven't?" I said sarcastically. "You're Mr. Perfect, huh?"

"I'm not saying that. It's just that I'm not . . ."

"You're not *what?*" I said, glaring at him.

He turned red and didn't answer.

"Handicapped?" I said. "Is that what you think I am, Hutch? Well, I'll show you how handicapped I am. I'm going down."

"C'mon, Luke . . ."

"I'm *going* down. You comin' or not?"

Hutch didn't answer, but when I started over the edge, he followed. I wasn't scared at first. I was too angry to be scared. All I cared about was proving that I could do it. It took a lot of concentration, too. There really wasn't much to hold on to, with my hands or my feet—just little ledges of rock an inch or so wide and an occasional root or twig. Sometimes the rock broke, or the twig came out in my hand. I was sweating with the exertion before long and, looking back, I guess I have to admit there was some fear in that sweat, too. Then I heard Hutch moan.

I looked over. He was clinging to the face of the mountain, his arms and legs both spread-eagled, and he was staring at the ground below. I looked down for the first time, too, and my stomach did a flip. "Man," I whispered. "It *is* pretty far, isn't it?"

"I can't move," said Hutch. "I'm too scared. My legs are starting to shake real bad, Luke."

I tore my eyes away from the ground and looked over at Hutch again. He was white as a sheet.

"Hey," I said, "look at me, okay?"

Hutch slowly raised his eyes to mine.

"That's it," I said. "That's cool." I made myself smile. "It's not that bad. Just don't look down. You wanna climb back up?"

"I don't think I can," said Hutch. "My arms feel like spaghetti."

"Okay. No problem," I said. "We'll keep going down. It's not really *that* far. Just move your left foot down real slow. There's a good-sized hunk of ledge just below you."

Hutch groaned again, but he started to feel for the toe-hold with his foot.

"That's it," I said. "Easy does it."

We moved down the face of the mountain, inch by inch, me talking Hutch all the way down. It seemed that we would never reach the ground, but finally we got close enough that I knew we were out of danger. I started to joke a little to try to get Hutch to relax. "Look at me," I said. I'd reached a wide ledge, and I turned and perched like a bird, swooshing my arms up and down. "See, I'm a bird."

"You're an idiot," said Hutch. But he smiled at least. He was feeling better. I could tell.

We climbed a little farther down, then I pushed off and jumped the last ten feet or so. "Geronimo!" I shouted.

Hutch thumped down beside me.

"That was some fun, wasn't it?" I said, once I caught my breath.

Hutch just shook his head. "Are you for real?"

"Of course I'm for real," I said. I was getting a rush by then. I'd done it! I'd really done it. I'd climbed down Top-o'-the-World! I got up and surveyed the face we'd just come down. I felt *great!*

"I'm going back up," I said.

Hutch blanched again. "No way," he said.

"Of course I am," I said. "The bikes are up there."

"We can walk around, Luke," said Hutch. "C'mon, don't be dumb. You proved your point, okay?"

I scowled at him. "It's not about proving anything," I said. "It's about having fun, feeling *free.* You can't tell me you didn't feel free up there?"

Hutch shook his head. "What are you talking about?" he asked. "Free from what?"

"From *everything!*" I shouted as I grabbed a handhold and hoisted myself up again.

The climb up was cool. I felt confident by then. I wasn't even afraid to look down. And I was able to notice how beautiful it was—the wind in my face, the valley below all gold and red. Once a hawk glided by, so close that I heard the rush of wind under its wings.

"Hey, brother," I called softly. "Look at me, up here with you."

I got to the top a long time before Hutch showed up and just sat there, feeling exhilarated. That's the best feeling, you know? When you're a little bit afraid of something and you conquer your fear and do it? The *best.*

When I got home that afternoon, my mom was in the kitchen, making spaghetti sauce.

"You're home early," I said.

"Yeah." She nodded. "I had a dentist appointment. What have you been up to?"

I popped an Oreo into my mouth. "Climbing Top-o'-the-World," I said casually.

She didn't seem to hear me at first. She gave the sauce a couple more stirs, then suddenly looked up. "Climbing what?" she asked.

"Top-o'-the-World," I repeated.

Her brows knitted together. "What do you mean, *climbing* Top-o'-the-World?"

I shrugged. "I mean going like this," I said, raking my hands through the air in an imitation of mountain climbing.

That *Oh-my-God!-You-could've-been-killed!* look was starting to creep into her eyes, and I was secretly enjoying it. Served her right, going behind my back and telling my friends to baby-sit me!

"You mean like mountain climbers do?" she asked.

I nodded.

"Up the face?"

I nodded again, waiting. By my calculations, it was j-u-s-t about time for her to say . . .

"Oh, my God! You could have been killed!" she blurted out.

I smiled, and that *really* got her going.

"Don't you smile at me, young man," she said, waving her sauce spoon around. "Don't you know how dangerous that was? What if you slipped? What if you fell?"

"I wasn't going to fall," I told her.

"But what if you did?" she kept insisting. "You would have been killed. Admit to me that if you fell, you would have been killed."

"Mom . . ."

"Admit it, Luke. I need you to admit it."

"I don't know."

"Luke. I've been up there. I know. You would have been killed."

"Maybe."

"Maybe? All right, let's go with maybe. You knew that if you fell, *maybe* you would have been killed, and you did it anyway? Why, Luke? Please tell me why?" She was getting a little hysterical, and I was starting to regret bringing the whole thing up.

"Calm down, Mom," I said. "I *knew* I wasn't going to fall, okay?"

She still didn't get it, though. I guess it's like when you're driving a car, and somebody thinks you're driving too fast, but you're behind the wheel and you know it's okay, but then when you're in the car and the other person is driving and they're going the same speed you were going, it feels like *they're* going too fast. You feel secure when you know you're in control. And when I was on the mountain, I knew *I was in control.* I wasn't going to fall. But I couldn't convince my mother of that.

"Just answer me this, Luke," she said at last. "Would you let Nick climb it?"

My brother, Nick, is thirteen and pretty well coordinated

for a kid that age, but I didn't have to think twice about whether I'd let him climb Top-o'-the-World.

"No," I told her.

"Why not?"

"Don't be stupid, Mom," I told her. "He might fall."

"Nick might fall, but you wouldn't?"

"That's right."

My mother sighed and shook her head. "Luke," she said quietly. (I really hate when her voice gets quiet. I know what's coming next.) "What you did today would have been foolish for anybody, but for you . . ."

I turned and walked away.

"Luke! I'm not through talking to you."

"Well, I'm through listening! Why don't you just get off my back!" I ducked into the bathroom, slammed the door behind me, and turned the shower on full blast so I couldn't hear her anymore. I pulled my clothes off, threw them in the corner, and climbed in, letting the warm water pour over me. After I calmed down a little, I felt kind of bad about the whole business. I try to be patient with my mom, you know, and with my dad, too. But they just really get to me sometimes.

A weird thing happened later that same night. God spanked me again. He has this habit of doing that to me when He thinks I'm out of line. Sometimes it's kind of subtle, and it takes a while for me to figure out He's doing it, but other times it's pretty obvious. This time it was so obvious it was disgusting. I turned on *Operation Rescue,* which is this TV show about rescuing people from tragedies, and who was on there but these two guys climbing a mountain. One of the guys was saying how he was a pretty good climber and there was no way he was going to fall, so of course you know he's going to. And he did. And of course my mother was sitting there watching it, too. Naturally she started right in.

"I hope you're watching this, Luke. See what I told you?"

I mean, I really felt like congratulating God on the subtlety, you know?

Anyway, this kid fell, and his friend climbed down and found him unconscious, so he put his hand under the kid's head, and all he could feel were the kid's brains.

To be honest, my stomach didn't feel too good when I heard that. I thought about Hutch and about how I'd made him climb with me. How would I have felt if Hutch had fallen?

My mom freaked when she heard the part about the kid's brains, too. "Did you hear that, Luke?" she said.

"No, Mom, I didn't hear it."

"Don't get wise, Luke. Do you believe me now about what could have happened?"

"Mom," I told her, "it's not like I didn't believe you before. It's just that I knew I wasn't going to fall."

My mom looked really frustrated.

"Luke," she said with this pleading look in her eyes. "You're part of a family. People love you. Don't you realize that if you get hurt, we all get hurt?"

I hate it when she says that. Of course I realize it. I remember how it was, how they were all those times

"Look, Luke," she went on. "I know you. I know if you want to climb a mountain, you're going to climb a mountain. All I'm asking is for you to get some safety gear and take some lessons first. Can you do that?"

"Yeah," I said. "I guess I can do that."

The kid with his brains falling out ended up being okay, which was some kind of miracle they said. But of course you knew he was going to be okay all along or they wouldn't have put him on *Operation Rescue,* right? What would be the point of showing you a rescue if the guy died? But I did join the outdoors club in school the next day. Not that I was worried about falling or anything, but I figured it was worth it if it got God and my mother off my back.

Wednesday, January 15

I broke up with Megan today, and I'm feeling kind of down about it. She called and wanted me to go get a soda, and I told her I couldn't—because, like I said, I want to cool it with her a little. So I told her I had to stay home and do homework, and she got annoyed.

"That's what you said last night," she said. "And the night before, too. Why do you have so much homework all of a sudden?"

"I don't know," I told her. "I just do."

"You can't take a break for an hour?"

"No, I can't. My parents are on my case about my grades."

"Why?" said Megan. "Are you doing bad?"

"No, I'm not doing bad. I'm just not doing as good as they want me to."

"Well, how bad are you doing?" she asked.

I was getting ticked off by then, because she was beginning to make it sound like I must be really stupid or something. So I didn't answer her, and there was this big silence on the phone. Finally, after we both got pretty tired of saying nothing, there was a loud sigh and Megan said, "You want me to come over and help you?"

Now, that really ticked me off—like she was so much smarter than me!

"No, I don't need any freakin' help," I said.

"Well, you don't have to be so mean about it," Megan snapped.

I didn't say anything again.

So Megan sighed again. "Why are you in such a lousy mood lately?" she asked.

"I'm not."

"Yeah, right. Be that way then. I'll just have to find something else to do tonight."

"Fine!" I said. "Why don't you give old Tony Lieberman a call? You seemed to enjoy sitting on his lap enough the other day while I was out in the ring getting the crap beat out of me."

There was another silence, then after a minute or two, in her most annoyed voice yet, Megan said, "Hey, don't try to pin that guilt trip on me, Luke. You got the crap beat out of you because you vegged out all Christmas vacation and you were out of shape."

Now, talk about ticking me off! It's bad enough to *know* that it's your own fault you got the crap beat out of you without having someone point it out to you. All that does is make you want to make up some other excuse as quick as you can and throw it back in their face.

"Oh yeah?" I said. "Well, maybe if you weren't bugging me to go out all the time, I might have had some time to keep myself in shape."

"Oh, is that so?"

"Yes, that's so," I said. "I really don't have time for all this dating right now anyway. Maybe we should just stop seeing each other for a while."

I figured she'd blow her stack then, but she didn't. She didn't say anything at all for a minute, and then she said, very calmly, "Well, fine then. Maybe I will go have a soda with Tony. Maybe he won't find it such a chore. Good-bye, Luke." Then she hung up.

Just like that. "Good-bye, Luke." I sat there and stared at the phone for about ten minutes, very confused. She didn't even sound all that upset. I mean, we gave each other Christmas presents! Didn't that mean anything? Here I am worrying all this time about breaking her heart, and she acts like it's no big deal. You know, you think you've got women figured out, and then they mess you up every time.

The worst part was, I was feeling *lousy*. I was feeling so lousy, I almost called her back to see why she *wasn't* feeling lousy. But then I figured that was stupid. I mean, this is what I wanted, right? This is exactly what I wanted. Now I can stop thinking about her all the time and concentrate on school and wrestling–and writing this stupid journal!

Friday, January 17

Well, here I am in my favorite spot again, staring at my favorite piece of torn wallpaper. Except I've made it a little more interesting to stare at because I drew a face on it: a little guy with a beard and sneaky eyes. Looks a little like the devil. Come to think of it, it looks more like Tony Lieberman. I can't believe what that creep did yesterday. He came up to me in the locker room and asked me if I'd *really* broken up with Megan. Actually, it was rather brave of him. I mean, I'd only broken up with her the night before. It was still a sore subject.

"What do you care?" I asked him.

"Well, I thought I might ask her out," he said.

I closed my locker and looked at him. "Ask her out? What do you mean, *ask her out?* I thought you two were just friends."

"We *were* just friends," he said, then he got this kind of weaselly little grin on his face. "But if you guys really aren't going out anymore, I wouldn't mind us being more than that."

"Oh yeah?" I sat down on the bench and started lacing up my wrestling shoes. I thought about Megan sitting on his lap that day. "Maybe you two've been more than friends all along," I said. "Maybe you've been jerking me around, huh?" I gave my laces a hard yank.

"What?"

Tony looked surprised, but surprised about what—

surprised that I'd accused him, or surprised that I'd caught him? Not that it really mattered anymore.

"No way, Luke," he was insisting. "We're buddies. I wouldn't move in on your girl. Honest."

I shrugged. "Doesn't matter anyway," I said. "She's not my girl anymore. Do what you want."

"You sure?"

"Yeah. I'm sure."

The truth of the matter is, I wasn't too concerned because I couldn't *really* see her going out with him. He's a good-looking guy all right, and he's nice enough, but he's not her type. He's kind of immature. I could see her being friends with him, because he's funny and all, but there's not much to him, not that I can see anyway. And Megan . . . Well, there's a lot to her. She thinks about things and cares about things, and she notices stuff that a lot of people don't notice, like the way the cloud shadows race across the valley on a windy afternoon, and how the woods smell like new life in the springtime, and . . . and how you shouldn't talk when things are too beautiful.

Now, Tony, he'd talk for sure. It's amazing how some people are. They can stand right in front of the most beautiful thing in the whole world and not even notice it. Even if you point it out to them, they're so wrapped up in themselves and what they're saying and doing, they still don't even notice. They'll say they do. They'll say, "Oh yeah," or, "Cool," or something, but they aren't really seeing the beautiful thing at all. That's the kind of guy Tony is.

Anyway, I figured Megan might go out with him once or twice, just to make me jealous, but nothing more than that. And then he comes back into the locker room again today, and I overhear him telling some guy how they went out and how she was so hot for him, and I'm thinking, What the hell is going on? I mean, she was never that hot for me. She never let *me* do anything. Not that I really tried. But still.

Anyhow, I don't much feel like writing tonight. I don't care whether I get into a good college or not. I don't care about much of anything. I can't even think of a word for how lousy I feel. It's weird how many things there aren't words for. I think I'll call Hutch, see if he wants to go get a pizza, maybe shoot some pool.

Saturday, January 18

Well, the good news is, today's meet got canceled because of a snowstorm, so I have another week to get myself back in shape. The bad news is, I'm grounded. I screwed up again last night.

I'd been doing pretty good, too—if you don't count climbing Top-o'-the-World, which was no big deal as far as I'm concerned, or chopping Daisy's tail off, which was an accident that could have happened to anybody. I hadn't even gone out drinking since the end of last summer down at the Cape, when a buddy and I snuck out after dark, had a few beers, and then took his boat out without any running lights and almost no gas, which is how we nearly got hit by the barge. Like I said, the weirdest things happen to me.

Anyway, Hutch came over last night, and we started talking about stuff, only not the stuff that was really on my mind. What was on my mind was Megan and Tony, and whether they were really doing all the stuff Tony said they were doing. I feel so confused about Megan now. Not that I think she's a bad person if she does it or anything. I mean, I know even nice girls do it, but, well, I haven't done it yet, you know? And when we were going out, she didn't act like she was expecting to do it, so I just got the idea that she hadn't done it yet either. Maybe it shouldn't be important, but I can't help it. It is.

Maybe Tony's lying. That's very possible. As I said before, guys do that. But then again, maybe he's not. I don't know why I care so much. I guess I get it from my parents. They're very old-fashioned that way. They still actually believe that people should wait until they're married to have sex.

Now, I'm no angel or anything. I'm not going to pretend I go around listening to every word my parents say or doing everything they tell me to do. I mean, I listen to them, but basically I make up my own mind about things. In this case, though, I can't seem to make up my mind. On the one hand, I think it would be pretty cool to have sex, but on the other, I don't want any diseases, especially AIDS. There aren't any second chances with AIDS, you know? It's not like you can say, "Gee, once I get over this I'll be more careful next time." I also don't want any kids, and it's not like a condom is the answer to everything, either. I mean, condoms break.

But then I sit down to watch TV, and I feel like I must be the only seventeen-year-old guy in the world who's still waiting. And sometimes it gets to me. Like last night. Hutch came over, like I said, and I was still feeling pretty mixed up and confused. This new show came on TV, so Hutch and I figured we'd check it out for a few minutes before we headed out to play pool. Next thing you know, this thirteen-year-old kid announces to his parents that he got this condom in school and that he can't wait to use it! And what does his mother do? She gives him a hug and says, all sweet and everything, "Oh, Joey. You're growing up."

She acted like it was nothing! Like he hadn't said anything much different from, "Look, Mom, I found a whisker on my face and I think I'm gonna shave." So I started thinking: Maybe my parents are the crazy ones—

nobody else seems to think it's any big deal. So I turned to Hutch.

"Hey, Hutch," I said. "Would your mother ever act like that if you told her you had a condom when you were thirteen?"

Hutch started laughing. "Yeah, right! She'd have a fit if she knew I had one now."

"Yeah." I laughed. "Mine, too."

"Good thing for dads, huh?" said Hutch.

"Yeah." I nodded. "Good thing for dads." *Not*.

I kept looking at Hutch then, wondering how many times he'd done it, wondering if I *was* the only seventeen-year-old guy on the face of the earth who hadn't done it. And I started to think that I really must be some kind of a freak. I mean, even supposing I decided not to do it until I was married, would there be any *girls* left who hadn't done it? What was the freakin' point?

"You got any on you?" I suddenly asked Hutch.

"What?"

I guess he was so wrapped up in the show, he'd forgotten what we were talking about.

"Condoms." I said. "You got any with you?"

"Well . . . yeah, sure," said Hutch. "Don't you?"

"I'm fresh out," I said. "Been a big month, you know? Holidays and all."

Hutch rolled his eyes and nodded, like it'd been a big month for him, too, and he got exhausted just thinking about it.

"Whad'ya say we go visit Lenny Bertoli up at the college and find us a couple of girls," I said.

"A couple of girls?"

"Yeah. I feel like doing it, you know?" Just hearing myself say that was pretty exciting. It felt kind of cool.

"Right now?" asked Hutch.

"Yeah. Right now." I suddenly stopped thinking about my parents and AIDS and stuff. All I could think about was doing it with some beautiful girl. That's how it usually happens when I screw up. I get these ideas and everything else kind of flies out of my head.

"I don't know," said Hutch. "It's getting kind of late."

Oh sure, I thought to myself. It's no big deal to him. He probably does it all the time anyway.

"And you've got a meet tomorrow," he reminded me. "Aren't you supposed to be in by eleven?"

"So, who said we have to stay late?" I told him. "We'll just run up there, find a couple of girls, do it, and come right back."

Hutch looked kind of doubtful about the whole idea. I figured he'd probably rather do it some other time, when he didn't have to rush so much, but I finally talked him into it.

So we went up to the state university, which is only about a half hour away, and found Lenny Bertoli, this kid from the wrestling team who graduated from our school last year. Nice guy, kind of quiet. We weren't really all that close, but close enough that he doesn't mind us coming up to visit him. He usually seems kind of glad to see us, in fact.

"Hey, Lenny," I said, when we got to his room. "How's it going?"

"Luke. Hutch," he said. "Hey. Come on in."

Lenny didn't look too great, to be honest. He looked

pale, and he had lost a lot of weight. His T-shirt could have really used a washing.

"Sit down," he said, pointing to his bed, which had these greasy gray sheets on it and smelled pretty bad. I glanced around the room for somewhere else to sit, but there wasn't any. The place was a mess, to tell you the truth, which was weird, because Bertoli used to be one of those real meticulous guys in high school, the kind who even keep their lockers neat. I guess he noticed me looking around, because he suddenly seemed embarrassed.

"Sorry about the mess," he said, sweeping a pile of books off a chair. "I've been meaning to do laundry and clean up some, but I've been real busy."

"Not a problem," I said. Hutch and I perched on the edge of the bed, and Lenny sat on the chair.

"So, how's it going?" I asked.

Lenny ran his fingers through his hair, which looked even greasier than the sheets. "Okay," he said. "How're things back home?"

"Good," I said. "Real good."

Lenny smiled, but his eyes looked sad. "How's wrestling going?" he asked me.

I shrugged. "Could be better," I said. "I got a little soft over the holidays."

Lenny nodded. "Yeah. That happens," he said. "Coach'll whip you back into shape. I miss that, believe it or not."

I wasn't sure, but for a minute, it almost looked like Lenny had tears in his eyes, which kind of surprised me. I didn't know wrestling had meant that much to him.

"Why didn't you go out for the team here?" I asked.

Lenny laughed softly. "Be real, Carver," he said. "This is the big time—Division One. You know I wasn't a star."

I shrugged. "So what? Everybody doesn't have to be a star."

Lenny cocked his head at Hutch. "Easy for him to say, huh?" he said.

Hutch nodded.

"So, how are your classes?" I asked, more to change the subject than anything. I wasn't feeling much like a star after last week's meet, and it was making me uncomfortable talking about it.

"Hard," said Lenny. "A lot harder than high school, but I'm hangin' in."

"That's good," I said.

We all nodded our heads and smiled.

"So," I said after a little more small talk, "what's going on around here this weekend?"

"Oh . . ." Lenny looked away, and his voice kind of trailed off. "Lots of stuff."

"Any parties?" asked Hutch.

"Oh sure," Lenny said quietly. "Always lots of parties." It was weird how he said it, though. Kind of sarcastic almost.

"Don't you like parties?" I asked.

Lenny looked at me and opened his mouth a little, like he was going to say something, but then he just sighed instead and smiled.

"Sure," he said, "parties are great. In fact, there's a big one over at Theta Xi tonight. Why don't you guys go."

"Why don't you come with us?" I said.

"Can't," Lenny said. "I've got a ten-page paper due."

"That bites," I said.

Lenny laughed. "Yeah, well, that's college," he said.

"You really *don't* like it, do you?" I asked.

Lenny shrugged. "It's just different from high school," he said. "Kind of big and impersonal. Nobody really even knows who you are."

"Yeah, so I hear," said Hutch.

Lenny looked pretty lost, and I felt bad for him. I tried to think of something to say to cheer him up. "It gets better," I said. "My sister used to feel the same way you do, but she loves college now."

Lenny nodded, but he didn't look all that convinced. Then suddenly he seemed to perk up again. "Hey, seriously," he said, "you guys go to the party. You drove all the way up here, and I can't hang out anyway. I've really got to get back to this paper. . . ."

"Well, if you're sure," I said.

Lenny nodded. "The place is right up the street," he said. "White house with big pillars out front. Just tell them you're freshmen, and they'll let you in. They don't know who the freshman are, and they don't really care, just as long as you pay your money and don't cause any trouble. You buy a cup for a few bucks, and you can fill it up at the keg all night long."

Hutch and I looked at each other.

"Well, I guess we might as well," I said, "seeing as we drove up here and all."

Lenny walked us downstairs to say good-bye and stood in the doorway, hands in his pockets, as we walked away. I looked back when we got down the street, and he was still standing there, leaning against the door frame. He looked small and lonely, under the bare, white lightbulb. I waved, but I guess he didn't see, because he didn't wave back.

The party had obviously been going on for a while by the time Hutch and I got there, and people were pretty drunk already. The room was crowded and dark. Hutch and I bought a couple of cups and filled them at the keg. Hutch chugged his in about a second and went back for another. I just sipped mine, though, because I promised my parents after that barge business that I wouldn't drink anymore, at least until I was out of high school. Besides, I was driving.

A DJ was playing somewhere in the back of the room, but nobody was really dancing yet. I looked around. The room was really huge and old-fashioned, with high ceilings. It looked like it might have been a mansion or something once, but now it was covered with cheap paneling and looked beat to hell.

"Hey," somebody shouted over the music, "I haven't seen you around before."

I turned. A cute girl with curly blond hair was grinning at me. Wow. This was going to be easier than I thought. I gave her a quick look up and down. She wasn't Megan, and she wasn't any movie star, but she would do. She had a nice smile and a body that was quite attractive, especially in the short skirt and tight, low-cut bodysuit she had on.

"I'm a freshman," I said. "Luke Brown." I thought it was probably a good idea not to use my real name.

"Hi, Luke. Sherry Keeler. And this is my friend Kate Samuels. We're sophomores, but that's okay. We like younger men." She winked and I laughed.

"I've got a friend here somewhere, too," I said, looking around. "Hey, Hutch," I yelled over the heads of the crowd. Hutch waved from across the room and started making his way through the tangled mass of people, trying not to spill his beer.

Hutch hit it off with Kate just fine, and he and I spent the next hour or so making up lies about what classes we were taking and stuff, and taking trips back and forth to the keg. I was pretending to drink, just to be sociable, but I kept spilling most of mine out when no one was watching. It didn't matter about the floor. It was already covered with beer anyway.

Hutch and Kate and Sherry were starting to get pretty drunk. It's amazing how silly drunk people look when you're not drinking. And there's another thing I've noticed about people when they drink: they get *very* friendly. The drunker Sherry got, the friendlier she got, until she was hanging all over me. Hutch and Kate started making out, but I really wasn't in the mood yet, so I asked Sherry if she wanted to dance. She said sure, so we made our way to the back of the room where the DJ was and where a bunch of people were crammed in all sweating together and calling it dancing. A slow song was playing, so Sherry put her arms up around my neck and laid her head against my chest, and we started to dance. She was dancing real close, and I could feel her body against mine, and it was pretty sexy, you know? Then she pulled my head down and started French kissing me right there on the dance floor! I was a little embarrassed at first, but then I noticed that half the other couples on the floor were doing the same thing, so I figured, What the heck? The thing was, it wasn't all that sexy anymore because Sherry's breath reeked, and I saw that her eye makeup had smudged all up on her eyelids. All of a sudden she didn't seem that attractive. I guess she was feeling pretty sexy, though, because she kept kissing me the whole rest of the song. And when the song ended, she whispered in this very husky voice, "Wanna go somewhere?"

I started to get nervous, because, well . . . like I said, I'd never done it before, and suddenly I wasn't so sure I even wanted to. I mean, part of me wanted to all right, but the rest of me was sort of chickening out.

"Uh, where would we go?" I asked her.

"How about your room?" she said. She really wanted to go, you could tell. Her eyes were half shut, and her lips were all puffy, and she was breathing heavy.

"Um . . . my roommate is doing a paper," I said.

"Well, my room then," she said. "I don't care where we go."

"How far is your room?" I asked.

You could tell she was starting to get annoyed. I guess guys usually jumped at the chance when she asked them.

"It's right over in Baker Hall," she said. "Is that too much of an inconvenience?"

"No," I said, although I had no idea where Baker Hall was. "No, that's fine."

"Well, then?" she said.

I looked at her face, which wasn't all that attractive anymore, as I said, but then I looked down at her body, which was still looking pretty fine, and I figured, What the heck. This is what I came here for, right?

"Okay," I said. "Just let me tell Hutch."

Hutch was still in a lip lock with Kate, and when I pulled them apart, he was so drunk that it took him a while to focus on my face.

"You better lay off the beer, Hutch," I told him. "You're getting wasted."

Hutch swatted at the air. "Imf-ine," he said, "Mine yerone biznez."

"Yeah, mine yerone biznez, y'old party pooper," Kate added, giggling.

That's the trouble with getting wasted, you know? You never realize you're wasted until you're wasted. I figured that was Hutch's problem, though. I had other things on my mind.

"Suit yourself," I said, then I pulled him aside. "Give me one of your condoms," I said.

He raised an eyebrow and tried to focus on me. "Whad ju say?"

I frowned. "You know what I said. Now don't make a scene, will ya? Just give me one."

"Wo-ho-ho," chuckled Hutch in what was supposed to be a whisper. "Lukie's got some action going. . . ."

"Shut up, Hutch," I said. "Just give me the damn thing."

Hutch finally stopped chuckling and wrinkled his brow like he was thinking and it was a real effort. "Um . . ." He burped. "I don't have any."

"What? You said you did."

"I did?"

"Yeah, back at my house, remember?"

"Oh yeah," he said, but I could tell he didn't remember a thing. Then he started to laugh. "Well, I lied." He laughed harder. He just thought he was the funniest thing in the whole damn world.

"Whasso funny?" asked Kate. He whispered in her ear, and they both burst out laughing. I left them there, hysterical together, and went to find Sherry again.

"Come on," I said when I found her. "Let's get out of here."

We walked about two blocks to Sherry's dorm. It was cold and icy out, and Sherry was staggering a lot. I looked at my watch. It was past ten already, and Coach had given us an eleven o'clock curfew. As captain I was supposed to set an example, too. I didn't want him to call and find me not home. It was a half hour drive back, and I had to get Hutch and all. . . . This wasn't working out. It really wasn't.

By the time we got to her room, I was feeling really nervous. It just didn't seem right anymore. Nothing seemed right. I guess it seemed right to Sherry, though, because as soon as we got inside her door, she threw her arms around my neck and started French kissing me again. Her hands started to slide down my chest, and suddenly I started to feel panicky. I looked into her face and realized that I didn't know her. I mean, I didn't know her *at all*. I didn't know where she came from, or what she cared about, or whether she liked cloud shadows or John Denver. Nothing. And suddenly it seemed all wrong. How could I do something so important, so *personal,* with someone I didn't even know?

I pulled away from Sherry and groped along the wall for the light switch.

"Whass wrong?" she asked, squinting in the sudden light. Man, she looked a mess. Her face was all red and puffy, and her makeup was smeared.

"I gotta go," I said.

"What? Why?"

"I . . . I forgot to bring a condom," I told her.

"Oh," she said. "Don' worry. I'm on the pill."

"But . . . like, what about AIDS and stuff?" I said.

She laughed and put her arms back around my neck. "I'm not worried," she said, rubbing herself against me. "Are you worried?"

She reached to switch the light off again, but I grabbed her hand. "Yeah," I said. "I am worried. Sorry."

"What?"

"Thanks, anyway, but I really gotta go."

"Thanks, anyway! Why, you li'l . . . ! What do you mean, you're worried? Are you ins-sinuating that I'm some kind of a slut or something! Are you . . ."

I didn't stay to hear the rest. I beat it out the door and back to the frat party as fast as I could. I found Hutch passed out and Kate nowhere in sight.

"C'mon, buddy," I said, shaking him awake. "Let's get out of here."

I basically carried him back to the parking lot and dumped him into the car, and then I wheeled out of there. I was doing about sixty on back roads all the way home, trying to beat the clock, and Hutch was getting thrown around a little. I mean, he had his seat belt on, but his head was flopping around like a rag doll's. Next thing I know, he started to moan.

"Hutch?" I said, "you okay? Hutch? Something wrong, buddy?"

And then I heard this god-awful sound, and I looked over. Hutch was retching all over himself and all over my dad's car!

"Damn, Hutch," I shouted. "Damn! Can't you open the window or something?"

But he couldn't even hold his head up. He just kept retching and retching, all over me, all over the car, until he passed out again. God, what a stench! It was all I could do to keep from retching, too. And the car! Damn. I looked up at the sky.

He'd done it again. God had spanked me again.

I'm really starting to wonder if the Big Guy's got it in for me. Sure seems like it sometimes. I mean, other kids get away with stuff all the time. Me, I step one foot out of line, and I get whacked upside the head. It doesn't seem fair.

Shoot. I need a break. I'm going to go find my little brother and see if he wants to wrestle.

Sunday, January 19

Another exciting day of being grounded. I'll bet I'm the world's leading expert on being grounded. Maybe I should write a book about it. *Luke Carver's Guide to Being Grounded.* I almost *could* write a book with all the writing I've done in this journal. I'm nearly up to a hundred pages! Amazing, huh? If anybody told me I'd ever write a hundred pages of anything in my life, I would've bet money they were wrong. This isn't like ordinary writing, though. It's like having someone to talk to—only maybe even better, because you can write just about anything, no matter how dumb it is, and you know no one's going to laugh at you.

Man, I still smell vomit. Ever since my parents made me clean up the car, I just can't seem to get the vomit stink out of my nose. Maybe I'll write about vomit. Ha ha. Seriously, though, it was a real experience cleaning that car. I could gag this minute just thinking about it. Cleaning up vomit has got to be a real test of how much you care about someone. I remember my sister did it for me once, back when I was younger. We were down at our beach cottage, and my parents were away for the night, so I went out on the beach with a bunch of my buddies and we polished off a bottle of vodka. I got wasted and got sick all over myself, but Kat took care of me and cleaned up after me and never said a word to our parents. She told me I was a jerk, and she told me if I ever did it again, she'd kick my butt, but she cleaned up after me and she never told. Kat's cool like that.

Anyway, like I was saying, I didn't really appreciate how much love it took for my sister to take care of me that way until I had to clean up that car. I do *not* love Hutch that much. I do not love *anybody* that much. I do not ever want to have to do that again as long as I live. I'm not even sure I'll love my kids enough to do that, although I guess I'll have to. Kids seem to retch a lot. I don't know how parents can put up with it. I guess they must get used to it after a while. Maybe they get broken in when their kids are babies, because babies just retch as a matter of course. It's kind of like a pattern with them: eat, retch, eat, retch, eat, retch. So maybe when they stop retching as a matter of course, the parents are so grateful that it's no big deal when they only retch once in a while.

I think I was an exception to that rule as a kid. I hardly ever remember retching, except one time when I was in the hospital. That was pretty cool, though, because it was just water—that sugar water they pump into your veins—and it didn't even taste bad coming up. I had to go to the bathroom, and I didn't know I was about to retch. My dad had to help me because I couldn't walk by myself. So he got me into the little stall, and he was in there with me because he couldn't let me go or I'd fall, and all of a sudden I started retching. And I mean gallons. They must've been pumping that stuff into me for days because it was shooting out of me like a fire hose, hitting the walls of the stall and splashing all over the place. I was getting soaked, but I didn't care because it felt really cool shooting out of me like that, and I was only wearing that little pajama thing they give you anyway. Finally it was over, and I felt sort of saggy and empty, like a deflated balloon.

"Thanks for the shower," my dad told me.

I couldn't see his face because of my bandages, but he took my hand and guided it along his chest and shoulders and head. Even his hair was soaking wet! And he was still just standing there, holding on to me like nothing had happened. I laughed so hard, I had to pee all over again.

Another funny thing happened in the hospital, too. They like for you to eat and drink a lot in there, so they had this refrigerator full of soda and Popsicles and ice cream and stuff out by the nurse's station. So one night my dad was staying over with me, and he'd made me eat about six cups of ice cream and drink a bunch of sodas. I got really full and tired, so I went to sleep. For some reason, my dad hadn't gotten to have any supper and he was starving, so he figured he'd sneak down to the refrigerator and get some ice cream and pretend it was for me, only he'd eat it. So he snuck down there and got himself this ice cream, and he snuck back all psyched because he finally had something to eat, only when he walks back into the room, who's there but the nurse taking my blood pressure.

They take your blood pressure about ten times a day, even if they have to wake you up to do it. So she's taking my blood pressure, and in he walks with the ice cream. Well, he got real embarrassed, because the ice cream was really there for the sick people, not the visitors, so he said, "Oh, hi. I was just getting this for him. He said he was hungry."

And I was lying there kind of groggy from the anesthesia

and from being half asleep, and I'm thinking, I don't remember wanting any more ice cream. But I guess if he was nice enough to go get it for me, I better eat it. So I sat up and reached my hand out. "Thanks, Dad," I said.

"Oh . . . yeah," he answered in this funny, surprised-disappointed kind of way. Then he put the cup in my hand. So I ate it while the nurse was puttering around in my room, and all the while my dad's not saying a word, and I'm thinking to myself, I'm *really* not hungry. I don't know why I asked for this. But I didn't want to hurt my dad's feelings because it makes him so happy to do stuff for me. So I forced it all down and went back to sleep, and I guess he never did get anything to eat that night. The next day I said to him, "You want to hear something funny? I can't remember asking you to get me that ice cream last night."

Dad starts cracking up and he tells me the whole story, and I start cracking up and the nurse walks in and wants to know what's so funny, so I tell her, even though my dad's trying his best to shush me. The nurse starts cracking up, too, and she goes out and comes back and gives my dad an ice cream, only the thing is, *he* isn't hungry anymore because he just went down to the cafeteria and had some breakfast. But he doesn't want to hurt the nurse's feelings, so as soon as she walks out of the room, he gives it to me, and I end up eating his stupid ice cream again!

I never realized how much they loved me until I was in the hospital that first time. I mean, I sort of knew it, the way all kids sort of know it, but I don't think I ever really *realized* it until then. I remember this one time, my mother was sitting in a chair by the side of my bed, working on some stitchery thing. I couldn't see her, but I could hear the push and pull of her needle. You get real good at hearing things when you can't see. And she was stitching away and talking to me, you know, like everything was fine, and I drifted off to sleep. I remember waking up again after a little while and not hearing the needle anymore. But I could hear her, crying softly.

I never let on that I'd heard her crying, but I promised myself right then and there that I'd never make her cry again. Which is why I feel so bad whenever I screw up. Every time it happens, I promise them, and myself, that it won't happen again. But it always does. Like Friday night. What a jerk I was—acting like I went up there to see Lenny, lying about who I was. Who was I anyway? I can't believe that phony was me. What if I had slept with that girl and she got pregnant? Or what if she had AIDS? What if I wrapped the car around a tree, flying home on those icy roads the way I did? I scare myself sometimes. I really do. I think I'm mature. I think I'm in control of myself. And then I go out and do stuff like that.

But then, on the other hand, I didn't sleep with her after all. And I didn't drink. So I could've done worse. Maybe I am getting better. Maybe I am getting more mature. I wish I knew for sure. It's pretty scary not knowing, especially when I think about graduating next year and going away to college. Then I'll be on my own, you know? And I'll have those kinds of temptations all the time. Sometimes I think life would be a lot easier if my parents would just ground me forever.

Monday, January 20

*I*t's weird, but I think this journal stuff is starting to be a habit. It's like whenever I'm really confused or upset about something, I find myself wanting to write about it. Like what happened in school today, right after fifth period. I was coming out of Mr. Hagerty's math class, when Mrs. Mellon, my guidance counselor, rushed by me.

"Can I have a word with you, Bill?" I heard her ask.

"Certainly," said Mr. Hagerty. "Is something wrong?"

"It's about one of your advisees from last year," said Mrs. Mellon. "Lenny Bertoli."

"Lenny Bertoli?" I said. "I know Lenny."

The guidance counselor looked at me then, like she hadn't really seen me before, and suddenly she stopped talking.

"That will be all, Luke," said Mr. Hagerty. "I'll see you tomorrow."

I nodded and walked out of the room, but by then I was curious, you know? So I stopped outside the doorway and listened.

"Suicide!" I heard Mr. Hagerty cry. "Lenny?"

A chill ran up my back.

"He's okay," Mrs. Mellon hurried on to say. "The attempt was unsuccessful. He's in the hospital. Very depressed, though."

I swallowed hard and stared at the floor. My stomach felt cold and fluttery. Lenny? Tried to kill himself? I thought back to last Friday, to the way his room looked, the way he was acting. I remembered him saying, "It's just different. . . . Kind of big and impersonal. Nobody really even knows who you are."

I thought about how lonely he looked that night. Jeez. Maybe Hutch and I should have stayed with him. Maybe we could have cheered him up or something.

"Luke?"

I looked up and there stood Megan, which was all I needed. As if I wasn't feeling lousy enough already. She had on the sweater I'd given her, too.

"What do *you* want?" I asked.

Megan frowned. "You don't have to be so nasty," she said. "I just thought maybe something was wrong. You look kind of pale."

She stared at me with those blue eyes of hers, which looked even bluer than usual. And for a minute, I almost felt like I was going to cry. I just wanted to grab her and hug her, you know? But I couldn't. So instead, I took a deep breath and tried to get a hold of myself. Then I steered her across the hall, away from Mr. Hagerty's open door.

"You remember Lenny Bertoli from last year?" I asked quietly.

Megan nodded.

"He's in the hospital. Tried to kill himself."

Megan's eyes went wide. "Oh no," she cried. "Why?"

I shook my head. "I don't know. I guess he was depressed about something. I saw him last Friday and he looked kind of down, but I never dreamed he'd do anything like that."

"That's so sad," said Megan. "Is he going to be okay?"

"I don't know," I said.

And I didn't know. I mean, it sounds like he's going to live. But is he going to be okay? That's a whole different question, isn't it?

Wednesday, January 22

*I*t's been a weird day. Really weird—so full of ups and downs, I feel like an elevator. It started out down, because I couldn't get Lenny out of my mind. I couldn't concentrate on anything in school. I just kept wondering what made him do it. I mean, sure he was homesick, but lots of kids get homesick when they go away to college, and they don't try to kill themselves. I wondered if he was flunking out or something. That would be pretty upsetting to a kid, especially with your parents paying all that money. But still, that didn't seem like enough to kill yourself over. Besides, Lenny was really smart in high school. I couldn't picture him flunking out. I felt like I should call him or something, but to tell the truth, I was afraid to. What do you say to someone who just tried to kill himself? It's kind of creepy, you know? What if you say the wrong thing?

Then around noon a big snowstorm started, and that took my mind off Lenny, because I started hoping we'd get out early. Only we didn't. So then I started hoping that practice would be canceled. Only it wasn't. But even so, I was *still* hopeful because I figured there'd probably be no school tomorrow. Might as well be optimistic, right?

The other thing that cheered me up was that I had the car, so I knew I'd get to drive in the snow. I looked forward to it all during practice. It was a little hairy when I actually got out in it, though. The roads were really slick, and the visibility was pretty bad, especially since it was dark by the time practice was over. There were a lot of cars off the road, out in the fields and everything, and that made me a little nervous. I didn't want to get into any more accidents, especially with the way my parents keep whining about our insurance rates.

Well, I skidded a few times, but I managed to pull out, and I made it up a couple of hills that other guys were backing down. I started to relax a little then, because I knew I had it under control. I love that feeling–when you're in a dangerous situation, but you've got it under control. Just like the way I felt when I climbed Top-o'-the-World.

The only thing that still had me a little worried was our mountain. The road up is a real bear, narrow and steep, with a hairpin turn and everything. I figured if worst came to worst, though, I could always park at the golf course down at the bottom and walk up, so I wasn't really sweating it.

Well, sure enough, I get to the foot of our hill and here's this guy backing down, and I think to myself, Should I try it or not? But of course I'm gonna try it, because I figure I'm a better driver than this guy. So I wait for him to get out of the way, and as I go by he rolls down his window and waves to me, but I figure he's just being friendly, so I wave back, then I swing in and start up. Well, I'm slipping and sliding a little, but I make the first leg of the hill okay, and I'm coming up on the hairpin. I gun it a little to get some momentum going into the bend and the back fishtails out, but I get it under control and I'm making it around, and I'm thinking, Yes! I *am* the world's best driver after all!

Once past the hairpin, I gun it again to get up some more momentum for the long, steep stretch ahead, when what comes looming out of the snow, broadside across the road about a hundred feet in front of me, but my next-door neighbor's Cadillac! Well, I hit the brakes and stopped in time, and that's when it dawned on me what the guy at the bottom of the hill had been trying to tell me. Nobody was going up that mountain until that Cadillac was out of the way.

I didn't care, though. I love helping people in distress, and my neighbor was obviously in need of help. It just made the whole adventure all the more exciting as far as I was concerned. I hollered to her that I'd be back as soon as I could, then I started backing down to find a safe place to leave the car.

Well, no sooner had I gotten around the hairpin than these headlights come right up behind me—and stop there. I shake my head and think, Who gave this guy a license? So I put my car in park and get out, figuring I'll have to point out to this bozo that, with all the snow, the road is only one lane wide, and in order for me to back down, *he's* got to back down. But believe it or not, it turns out that the headlights belong to a pickup truck, and behind the wheel is a guy in a cowboy hat. That really surprised me because, on the whole, guys with cowboy hats and pickup trucks are pretty good drivers. Well, I figure he must be confused or something, so I knock on his window and say, "Excuse me, but I'm trying to back down."

At which point the guy rolls down his window, looks at me, and says, "Nice going, asshole."

Now, like I said, I don't punch people anymore, but for a minute there, I was very tempted.

"Pardon me?" I said, giving him the benefit of the doubt in case he wanted to change his attitude.

"I said, nice going, asshole," he repeated. "Don't you know better than to stop in the middle of a hill!"

My hands were squeezing into fists, and I was really, *really* starting to get the old urge to swing them, but I was cool. I was cool.

"If you'll just let me back down," I told him, "I'll get out of your way, and then you can take your four-wheel drive truck right up around the bend and over the Cadillac that's broadside across the whole road up there, okay, pal?"

He didn't say anything then, just glared at me for a while, like somehow this whole situation *had* to be my fault. Then he grunted and said, "Well, I ain't goin' anywhere until *somebody* gets *him* off my tail." He jerked his thumb over his shoulder at yet another car that had come up behind us while were talking. Since it was quite obvious that Mr. Cowboy Hat was not about to inconvenience himself any more than he'd already been inconvenienced, and since I was the only other "somebody" in the immediate vicinity, I figured it was up to me to go back and explain the situation to the new guy, who turned out, to my relief, to be a normal human being and immediately started backing down.

I grinned at Mr. Cowboy Hat as I walked by, and he called me a *flaming* asshole. I wasn't mad anymore, though, just amazed and a little bit amused. I mean, here was the proverbial black pot if ever there was one. So I didn't answer. I just shook my head, which seemed to infuriate him more than anything I could have said. As soon as the other car was out of his way, he made a great show of flying down the hill in reverse, then slamming into forward and spinning his wheels as he roared off into the storm.

I shook my head once more, then backed down and parked at the golf course. I shouldered my book bag and started up again on foot. It was slow going because the wind was strong and the snow was right in my face, plus there was a glaze of ice under the new snow that even made walking tricky. Meanwhile, cars keep passing me by, zigging and zagging their way up the hill despite my efforts to flag them down and warn them. By the time I got up as far as the hairpin, it looked like a spinout at the Indy 500. There were cars all over the road, frontward, backward, sideways. . . . By some miracle, though, it didn't seem that any of them had plowed into one another, just into the snowbanks on the sides of the road. With the cars were an assortment of owners, pushing, pulling, swearing, spinning their wheels, or just standing there, staring at their cars as if waiting for them to get themselves out. Obviously, "somebody" had to take charge. Ah, I thought to myself. Here is a job for a flaming asshole!

I ditched my book bag in the snowbank and started helping the first car I came to, which was a little sports car that'd done a 360 and ended hung up on the bank with its drive wheels in midair. The lady driver was pretty shook up and obviously wasn't going to be much help, and strong as I am (and I like to think I'm pretty strong), I knew I wasn't going to be able to get her out alone.

"Hey!" I shouted to a couple of guys a little farther up the hill. "Wanna come on down here and give me a hand with this one? Then I'll come up there, and we'll get you guys out."

I guess that made sense to them, because they came right down. The next thing I knew, some of the other people came down, too, and then everybody else quit working on their own cars and joined in. Together we lifted the front end right up off the bank and walked it around and put it down on the road again. It was so cool!

"Park down at the bottom of the hill," I told the lady, "and don't let anybody else up till we send word that we've gotten the road open." She nodded and took off, and the rest of us went on to the next car. Before long we were having a grand old time, laughing and joking, forgetting the cold and the snow, just having fun helping one another.

An hour or so went by, and then my dad and Nick came down the hill on Nick's quad, looking for me. When they saw what was going on, they both pitched in, too. My dad helped with the cars, and Nick started ferrying the stranded people up the hill on the quad. Then he went around the neighborhood gathering some of his friends with their quads, and pretty soon it was starting to feel like a carnival out there. It reminded me of the year that a hurricane hit our summer house down at Cape Cod, and all the neighbors pitched in to help clean up. It's amazing how nice people turn out to be when problems like that come along.

Or, I should say, *most* people. Just as we got the Cadillac out and sent word down that the road was open, guess who comes roaring up around the bend? Yup, good old Mr. Cowboy Hat. I straightened up when I saw him, watching to see if he was going to stop and lend a hand or anything, but he just kept on coming, shooting snow and slush all over everybody in his path. I had this shovel in my hands, you know, and I found myself squeezing the handle real tight as he came closer. What I wanted to do was bash it right across his windshield. But I didn't. I just stood there giving him hard eyes. He flipped me the bird as he went by, then gunned it up the hill and around the bend.

"Damn!" I said to the man beside me. "Did you see that?"

The man just shook his head. "Let it go, son," he said. "People like that are their own worst enemies."

I thought about that for a minute, and then I nodded. "Yeah," I said, "I guess you're right." I plunged my shovel back into the snow and took out my anger on the storm. Finally, the last car was out and safely parked down at the golf course, and the last neighbor was ferried home. I was cold and tired, but I felt good. Real good.

Mom had kept dinner warm and had hot chocolate on the stove when we came in, so we all sat around and ate and drank, telling the whole story over from beginning to end, everyone laughing and talking at once. Mom listened and listened, laughing out loud when we told about how dad had slipped and fallen flat on his back in a puddle of slush. Then she grew quiet when I told about the man in the cowboy hat.

"I'm really proud of you, Luke," she said, "holding your temper like that. It takes a lot more guts than fighting."

That's when I got the knot in my stomach, and all the good feelings melted away.

"I gotta get going," I said, pushing myself away from the table. "I got a lot of homework to get done."

Now I'm sitting here, feeling down again, thinking about what my mom said about fighting, and about Mr. Cowboy Hat and me, and ~~the day that I got hurt~~ why things turn out the way they do. It seems unfair sometimes, but other times I'm not so sure. Because the thing is, if I'd kept going the way I was going a few years back, I probably *would* have punched out Mr. Cowboy Hat today. Come to think of it, if I'd kept going the way I was going, I might have *been* just like Mr. Cowboy Hat by now.

Friday, January 24

*I*t's almost midnight, but I can't sleep. My guts are hamburger. I screwed up again, BIG TIME. I'm still shaking thinking about it. I'm starting to get really worried. What's happening to me? Why do I keep doing these things? I mean, I've always been a bit of a screw-up, but lately it's like one thing after another. And tonight . . . tonight was the worst ever.

There was a pep rally at school for the meet tomorrow, and I had to go because I'm the captain, but I'm still supposed to be grounded, so my parents told me to go to the pep rally and come straight home afterward. I told them I would, and I meant to. I really did. But the thing is, the pep rally got over early. And then Hutch and a couple of the other guys asked me for a ride to this party they were going to, and I know I should've said no, but I hate saying no to people, especially my friends. Besides, I figured, What's the harm? I could give them a ride and still be home by ten o'clock, which was when my parents were expecting me anyway, and everybody would be happy, right?

Wrong. Hutch no sooner got into the car than he pulled out a flask and started passing it around.

"Hey, you guys," I said. "Cut that out. The last thing I need right now is to get caught with liquor in the car."

"Aw, have a slug and calm down," said Hutch, pushing the bottle toward me across the seat.

I knocked it away. "What do you think I am," I said, "a dickhead like you?"

"Whoa." Hutch raised his eyebrows. "Cranky, cranky. Could it be you're so cranky because Megan's going to be at the party tonight, and you're not?" Hutch passed the bottle over to the backseat, turned up the volume on the radio, and hit the scan button.

"Don't worry, Luke," my friend Terry yelled from the backseat. "We'll look after her for you, won't we, guys?"

"Yeah, yeah," they all yelled. "We'll be glad to look after her, Luke."

"Shut up," I shouted over the radio. "You're all a bunch of dickheads."

They laughed.

"Oh, wait! Wait! I love that song!" Terry jumped up and leaned over the seat, reaching for the buttons on the radio. His elbow hit me in the face, and the car swerved.

"Damn it!" I shouted. "Sit down, will you!"

"Aw, chill out!" yelled Terry, and he whacked me on the back of the head just as I was coming to a stop sign. I slammed on the brakes, and he sort of fell forward into my lap, and then there was all this confusion. I guess my foot got knocked off the brake and we started rolling again, because the next thing I knew, there was this jolt and then an awful scraping sound. I shoved Terry out of the way just in time to see this car going by right in front of my nose.

"Oh, God, no," I screamed. "God, NO!"

"What?" shouted Hutch. "What happened?"

"We just hit that car," I said.

"How do you know we hit him?" asked Terry. "Maybe he hit us."

"He's got the right-of-way, you asshole!" I shouted.

"Goddamn, what am I going to do now?" I broke out in a sweat. "I'm not even supposed to be over on this side of town!"

The other car had gone a little way up the road and had pulled over. I put my head down on the steering wheel, and tears sprang to my eyes. I couldn't believe it! How could this be happening? I was in so much trouble already. How in God's name was I going to face my parents? My heart was pounding, and my legs started to shake.

"We got trouble, Luke," said Hutch.

I looked over at him. "You think I don't know that?" I said.

"No, I mean more than you think." He held up the liquor bottle.

"Oh, God! I forgot about that." I looked over at the other car. A man had gotten out and was checking out the damage to the side of his car. He turned and started walking our way. Fear grabbed me by the throat and started choking me. Suddenly, I couldn't face it–any of it. The man, the cops, *my parents.*

"We gotta get out of here," I said, and I stepped on the gas.

"What!" Hutch yelled. "Luke, what are you *doing?*"

I sped down the street and veered off the main road onto a side street. "Ditch that bottle!" I yelled.

"But . . ."

"Just ditch it!"

Hutch started to open his window.

"No, wait," I said. I turned down another side street and pulled over. "Get out," I said, my voice trembling.

"What?" they all yelled.

"GET OUT, ALL OF YOU!" Tears were streaming down my face by then, and I was shaking so bad, I could hardly talk. The rear door opened, and the guys in the back climbed out.

"Luke," said Hutch. "What are you gonna do?"

"I don't know," I said, grabbing him by the shirt and shoving. "Just get *out*!"

"Okay, okay." Hutch opened his door. "But you gotta go back, buddy. You gotta."

"Don't tell me what I gotta do!" I cried. "You bastards got me into this!" I leaned over and pulled the door shut, then stepped on the gas and roared away.

I wound my way through a couple of more side streets, my hands clenching the steering wheel, my guts in a knot. I felt sick—I mean really sick, like I might throw up. It was slowly dawning on me what I'd done. I'd run from the scene of an accident. I hadn't stopped to see if anybody was hurt. I'd just run. I was crying so hard, I could hardly see to drive.

"God, help me," I cried. "God. *Please*. Help. Me."

Then I thought of something, something really stupid, but that's how whacked out I was. I thought maybe I could deny the whole thing, pretend it never happened. I pulled over again and got out to look at the front of my car.

It was a mess. The bumper was torn off, the whole left fender was crushed in, and the hood was crumpled. Any glimmer of hope that I might have had faded. I just stood there staring at it, feeling like someone was slowly shoving my guts through a meat grinder.

"You idiot," I said to myself. "You fool. Did you actually think there was a chance in hell that *you* could get away with *anything?*" I looked around me at the strange neighborhood, the house windows glowing yellow and warm, the people inside going about their ordinary routines, oblivious to me standing outside in my private hell. Suddenly, all I wanted was my own home and my own family close around me.

And in that moment, I knew I had to go to the police. I was scared shitless. But if I ever wanted to be able to go home again, I had no choice.

I got back into the car and turned it around. Slowly, like a zombie, I drove, numbly retracing my route. I got to the main road again and pulled out. Almost instantly I heard the wail of a siren, and then a second later there were flashing red lights behind me. I swallowed hard and pulled over.

The cop approached carefully with his hand on his gun. He stopped a ways back and shined his flashlight into the car. I rolled down my window, and he pulled out his gun. I put my hands up, and he came forward and yanked my door open.

"Out of the car," he said.

I got out, and he shoved me roughly toward the front of the car.

"Hands on the hood," he said, "feet spread."

I did as he said and then stared at the sky, trembling while he frisked me.

Why, God? I asked in silence, dried tears itching on my cheeks. WHY?

"You involved in an accident at the intersection of West and Main?" he asked.

"Y-Yes, sir."

"You run from the scene?"

"Y-Yes."

"Why?"

"I w-w-was"—my lips trembled so badly, I could hardly get the words out—"s-s-scared."

"Scared of what?"

"I've . . . only had my l-license a year," I blurted out. "I've gotten two tickets and been in t-two accidents, and I'm in trouble with my parents already. I wasn't even s-supposed to be out driving around tonight. I'm grounded."

The cop stared at me a long time.

"Do you know how serious running from the scene of an accident is?" he asked.

I nodded. "I-I think so."

"If there are injuries," the cop said, "you could go to jail."

My heart banged and tears stung my eyes again. Oh, God. *Oh, God, no, please.* "Do you . . . know if there are injuries?" I croaked.

"Not yet," said the cop. "The call was just coming in when I spotted you turning out of that side street."

He shined his flashlight into the car again.

"The report said there were several passengers in the car," he said.

I hung my head. "There were," I said. "I threw them out."

"Why?"

"They were . . . drinking."

The cop gave me a sharp look. "Were you?"

"No, sir. I was trying to get them to stop when the accident happened."

The cop pulled a piece of chalk from his pocket and drew a line on the ground.

"Walk it," he said.

I walked it while the cop continued to stare at me.

"I wasn't drinking," I repeated.

He nodded, then checked my license and registration and did a thorough search of the car. "All right," he said. "I believe your story. Get into your car. I'm going to let you follow me down to the station."

"Yes, sir," I said.

"I know who you are and where you live," he said, "so don't even *think* of trying to make a break for it."

I shook my head wearily. "I won't," I promised.

When we got to the station, the cop made me call my parents. All I really remember of the conversation was my dad yelling, *What!* about a million times. I waited in the cop's office for them to come, and the cop read me all the statutes about leaving the scene of an accident. He still wouldn't tell me whether there were injuries or not, and all I could think of was going to prison, being locked up, and not being allowed to leave. Not being able to live with my family, to spend time with my friends, not being home for the holidays, not having Daisy sleeping by my bed.

I started shivering again and couldn't stop. I put my

head down in my hands. That's how I was when my parents walked in.

I looked up at them and then looked away. I'd seen that frightened, bewildered look in their eyes too many times before. They were pale and rumpled. I'd gotten them out of bed.

The cop thanked them for coming and gave them a quick rundown of the facts. They assured him quietly that we had insurance and would take full responsibility for everything that had happened. Then the cop left to check on the status of the victim and his car.

The room was silent after he left, and I could no longer avoid looking at them. My mother was standing by the window, staring out. The venetian blinds painted stripes of light on her face, and the reflection of the streetlight shone in her watery eyes. My father sat bowed over in a chair, staring at his clasped hands.

"I'm sorry," I whispered hoarsely.

They both looked at me, but neither of them said anything. I knew why. "Sorry" loses its meaning when you've heard it a hundred times. I put my head back down into my hands again.

The cop came back in and sat down behind his desk. We all looked at him, and I, for one, held my breath.

"No injuries," he said.

My breath whooshed out.

"Thank God," my mother said.

"I believe," the officer went on, "that what we have here is a typical teenage panic attack. Your son seems to be a decent kid—respectful and remorseful. I think he learned a lesson here tonight, and I doubt he'll make this type of mistake again. I told all that to the victim."

The cop looked directly at me then. "You're a lucky young man," he said. "The victim turned out to be a decent guy. Based on what I told him, he said he's not going to press charges. You're free to go."

I slouched back into my chair, weak with relief.

My father and mother came forward to shake the officer's hand and thank him. I thanked him, too.

He smiled. "See," he said to me, "cops aren't so bad."

"No, sir," I said. "They're sure not."

"All right," he said, handing me back my keys. "Just don't ever give me any reason to regret going easy on you."

"I won't, sir," I said, tripping over my chair in my haste to get out of the station. "I promise. I won't."

My parents walked silently beside me to the parking lot. My father slowly circled the car, surveying the damage, his lips pressed into a thin, hard line. He heaved a great sigh, then came over and stood beside my mother and me.

"I don't know what to say to you, Luke," he said. "I don't know what goes on in your head. I don't know where it's all going to end."

I swallowed hard to keep the tears inside. I wanted to tell them again that I was sorry, tell them again that there wouldn't be a next time. No more drinking, no more speeding, no more taking stupid chances, no more sneaking, no more broken promises. But it was no use. When trust is gone, words are no good.

Saturday, January 25

I just got back from the meet. What a disaster. I don't know whether it was because of last night, or because I kept remembering how disappointed everyone had been in me the last time, but I was a wreck, right from the start. I just wanted to win so badly, wanted to prove that there was *something* good about me, *something* to be proud of. But I was so scared of losing. It never seemed to matter so much.

At first I was busy, helping with the weigh-ins, leading the warm-ups, and all that. But then the matches started, and I was sitting there looking around and I saw that Hutch and all the guys were there. They were grinning at me and giving me the thumbs-up sign and trying to let me know that they were there for me and that they were sorry about last night. And my mom and dad were there, too, in spite of everything. They weren't talking to me, but they were there, and my brother was, too. And then in walked Megan with Tony. Megan saw me looking at her, and she smiled and waved; her lips formed the words, "Good luck." Somehow that hurt even more, because I could see that she wasn't hurting. I guess that meant I never mattered to her as much as I thought I did. And that made me mad, made me want to win all the more, to show her, too, that there was *something* good about me, *something* worth missing.

Then the other team came out and started their warm-ups. I scoped out the big guys, looking for the biggest; I found him, and he was *big*. I couldn't really tell how much muscle he was carrying, though, because he still had his warm-up suit on. He had a pretty thick neck, though, and that was enough to start me worrying.

When the meet started, I tried hard to concentrate on what was going on, but I just kept thinking about last night and about how much I'd been screwing up lately. And then I started thinking about how bad I'd gotten beat at the tri-meet. And the more I thought, the more nervous I got. Even though I knew Coach'd worked me extra hard since the tri-meet, and even though I'd been lifting an awful lot, I still wasn't sure I was back in peak condition yet. And then I started to think, What if I lose again? What will I have left if I can't even hold my head up as a wrestler?

That's when I broke out in a sweat. And then it was all over. I couldn't concentrate, couldn't even keep track of what was going on out there on the mat, couldn't hear anything but the blood pounding in my own ears. Coach had to come over and give me a shake to remind me when it was my turn to loosen up.

"What?" I looked up at him in surprise. "What?"

He got right down into my face then. "Where's your head today, Carver?" he said. "Get back there and loosen up!"

Somehow I got my warm-ups off, somehow I got my headgear and mask on. I started dancing around behind the bench, but then I looked over and saw that Thick Neck had his warm-ups off, too—and he looked like he was wearing a full set of football pads under his skin. My guts turned to ice.

Coach knew. He took one look at me, and he *knew.* "Pull yourself together, Carver," he said in a low voice. "It's all tied up. The meet is riding on you."

Just what I needed to hear! I stumbled out onto the mat, and my cheering section started in. "Car-ver! Carver!" I sucked in a big breath and tried to calm myself, then bent over, eye to eye with Thick Neck. We shook hands, the ref blew the whistle, and we started circling. Normally I'm okay once the whistle blows. Some kind of a sixth sense kicks in, and I forget about the crowd, about winning or losing, about everything but me and the guy I'm staring down. But I couldn't focus, couldn't think. I kept looking for a chance to shoot, but I couldn't find one. Then everyone in the stands started yelling, "Shoot! Shoot!" And then I panicked and shot—too soon, too sloppy. He sprawled and I fell and he came down on top of me. I fought to keep my arms tight, but he peeled one of them free and pulled it over my back until I had no choice but to go with it. Then he threw all his weight on top of me and went for the kill.

"Arch! Arch!" everybody was screaming. "Fight!" And I arched, and arched, and arched, until every pore of my body was screaming in pain and my head felt like it was going to blow right off. But he was merciless, driving and driving, until I heard the ref's hand smack the mat and the whistle blew. A groan went up from the stands, and it took all the strength I had left to haul myself up and stand there while the ref lifted the other guy's hand in the air.

Coach gave me a halfhearted swat on the rear as I came off, but he didn't look at me. And I couldn't blame him. I couldn't look at my parents or my friends or . . . anyone. I kept my mask on, hiding inside it when we went out to shake hands with the other team, then I bolted for the locker room. When I got to the gym door, though, someone was blocking the way. Megan, of all people! I put my head down and tried to step around her, but she moved again to block my path.

"What is it?" I asked her. "What do you want?"

"I want to know what's going on with you, Luke," she said.

She didn't say it mad or anything. She said it like she cared. And I looked up then, into her eyes, and I got that feeling like I was going to cry again. I wanted more than anything to tell her what was going on with me, because if anyone would understand, I knew she would. Only I couldn't tell her, because I didn't understand myself.

And then Tony walked up and put a hand on my shoulder and said, "Tough break, Luke. Sorry."

I looked at him standing there, and all I could think of was him holding Megan—you know, the way I wanted to hold her at that minute. And I got so angry, I wanted to punch him right there, wanted to punch him so bad that I got scared that I might. When I finally pushed past Megan and walked away, I was shaking.

Saturday, February 8

This is rich-me writing when nobody is making me. Robinson sent a note home that I could be excused from the journal assignment, and I'm doing it anyway, because I want to. Who'da thunk it, huh? I found the journal today under a pile of clothes on my chair, and I sat down and started looking through it. It was weird reading it again, kind of like watching an out-of-control freight train barreling straight toward

Saturday, February 8

This is rich—me writing when nobody is making me. Robinson sent a note home that I could be excused from the journal assignment, and I'm doing it anyway, because I want to. Who'da thunk it, huh? I found the journal today under a pile of clothes on my chair, and I sat down and started looking through it. It was weird reading it again, kind of like watching an out-of-control freight train barreling straight toward a cliff. It was strange to see all the stuff I'd crossed out, too. Maybe Mrs. Robinson was right: maybe writing is a good way to get to know yourself. Maybe that's why I want to keep doing it. There's an awful lot I still don't understand. Besides, there's not a heck of a lot else I can do right now.

So, where to begin? Jeez. Where I left off, I guess, that afternoon after the meet. Seems like so long ago, it's hard to believe it's only been two weeks. It has, though. Two very long weeks.

I was alone in the house that afternoon. My parents went out shopping, Nick was over at a friend's, and Kat was away at school. It was just me and the silence—*again*. I can still remember that silence. It was the kind that presses down on you and chokes your breath out. I'd known that silence all too well, recovering from my surgeries. And this time, it wouldn't go away, no matter how loud I turned the stereo up. Plus, everywhere I looked there were eyes staring back at me: Megan's at the meet that morning, Coach's in the locker room afterward, my parents' at the police station the night before. Only one sound broke the silence, echoing on and off inside my head–the sound of the groan that went up in the gym that morning when the whistle blew.

I wanted to take my dirt bike out and ride as fast and as far as I could–feel the wind in my face and the power of the engine winding out underneath me. But you can't ride a dirt bike in the snow. I couldn't stay in, though. Couldn't stay and listen to the silence one more minute.

"C'mon, Daisy," I said, "let's take a walk."

Daisy leaped for joy, like I'd just made her the happiest dog in the world, and we headed out across the backyard.

The sun was out and the temp was in the thirties, which felt almost springlike after all the cold we'd had. I was sweating in my heavy coat before long, so I took it off and hung it on a branch where I could pick it up on the way back. Then I headed into the woods. Daisy ran ahead, wagging her stub of a tail.

There were several trails to choose from, all packed down nice and hard by the snowmobiles. I chose the lower trail, the one that winds down the mountain, past the pond, and into the pine forest. The snow wasn't as thick there. It never is. The pines catch a lot of it on the way down. The pine needles made a spongy cushion under the snow and my steps made no sound. Everything was hushed, like an empty church with the lights off. It usually soothes me to be there, smoothes away my rough edges. But not that day. That day, the hush only seemed to add to the weight of the silence. I remember feeling so lost, wondering why my life seemed to be coming in for a crash landing. Megan, my parents, my wrestling . . . I was failing everybody and everything I cared about.

I don't think I knew at first where I was heading. I just kept moving, putting one foot in front of the other, following the trail. Before I knew it, I came to Snake River, gurgling cold and black between banks mounded over with snow. The trail follows alongside it through the gorge, then south along the back side of the mountain, and I just kept following the trail. At last I came to a familiar little footbridge that crosses over a narrow part of the river. Only then did I realize where I'd been headed all along. Over the river, beyond the bridge, was Megan's house.

Megan was out in her backyard, brushing her horse. Horses are about the only thing she and I never really saw eye to eye on. She loves horses and I love dirt bikes, and although we both love the woods, horses and dirt bikes don't mix. Not that the dirt bikes give a hoot about horses, of course, but horses really *hate* dirt bikes. It was no big deal, though. We both liked hiking anyway.

While I was standing there, watching Megan, Daisy came loping out of the woods. She immediately started wiggling all over and whining because she wanted to run right over the bridge and say hi to Megan. I grabbed her collar and held her back, though, because I wasn't sure I wanted to say hi. I wasn't sure why I was there at all, except maybe I just wanted to look at Megan or be near her or something.

I stayed back in the woods behind the trees and made Daisy lie down, and I just went on watching for a while. I mean, not like a pervert or anything. I was just trying to figure out what I was feeling. Because the thing was, I broke up with her so it wouldn't end up being hard to break up with her, you know? But it was being hard anyway. Wicked hard.

I watched her stretching up on her toes, brushing her horse's back, smoothing, combing, quietly talking to him, and I started wishing I were a horse. Then she bent over, and her long hair fell forward and rippled in the sunlight like a copper-colored waterfall. And I wanted to hold her again and tell her that I . . . that I . . . I guess I didn't really know what I wanted to tell her. That was my problem.

Someone shouted hello, and Megan straightened up and looked toward her driveway. I looked, too, and who came riding up, on a *horse* of all things, but Tony! Can you believe it? The guy had a horse! I figured he probably went out and rented one just to impress her. What a phony!

Megan put her brush down and climbed up on her horse, too. She walked the horse over toward Tony, and the two of them talked for a couple of minutes while their horses nuzzled each other. How *sweet*, I thought, wanting to gag. Then Megan swung her reins around, and the next thing I knew, they were both walking their horses right toward me!

Now, the last thing I wanted was for them to see me hiding there in the woods, spying on them like some sort of pathetic freak, so I jumped up into the nearest tree and started climbing as fast as I could, getting scratched and poked like crazy because the nearest tree turned out to be an old prickly pine. It was nice and thick, though, so I felt pretty safe up there, out of sight. That is, until I looked down and saw Daisy standing at the bottom staring up at me and wagging her stumpy tail!

"Oh jeez," I whispered. "Go on, Daisy. Go away. Go home!"

She stopped wagging her tail and cocked her head at me in confusion.

"Daisy!" I suddenly heard Megan cry. "What are you doing here?"

With a joyful yclp, Daisy bounded out from under the tree. Through the thick maze of branches, I could see her pale form dancing around Megan's horse.

"Hello, Daisy! Hello, girl!" Megan squealed. "What were you doing in there, chasing a squirrel? Did you come all this way to visit me by yourself? What a good girl."

"Who the heck is Daisy?" Tony asked.

"Luke's dog," said Megan. "She used to follow him over all the time when he'd come to see me on his dirt bike. I can't believe she came by herself, though. It's about a three-mile trek."

"Luke?" she yelled, twisting first this way, then that, in her saddle. I flattened myself against the trunk, sweating bullets. Thank God the trail was all trampled and muddy from the horses, so she couldn't see my footprints. I don't know what I would have done if she'd gotten down from her horse and started looking around. Flung myself out of the tree and killed myself, I guess.

Megan turned toward the trail and yelled out my name again.

"I'll bet Daisy ran on ahead," she told Tony. "Luke must be on his way over. We'll probably meet him on the trail."

Tony grunted like he was real thrilled with that news.

"Come on, Daisy," Megan called. "Let's go find Luke."

Daisy let out a joyful bark and bounced down the trail ahead of the horses.

"What happened to her tail?" I heard Tony ask.

"Oh," Megan giggled. "You won't believe it. Luke chopped it off."

"No way! By mistake or on purpose?"

"By mistake, silly. He was chopping wood."

"No way." Tony burst out laughing, and then Megan joined in. They disappeared around a bend, but their laughter still rang in the air.

Anger burned its way up my throat. Anger and humiliation. What was wrong with those two, laughing over something like that? I'd have expected as much from Tony. But from Megan? I made a fist and smashed my hand against the tree trunk.

Sunday, February 9

I had to quit writing yesterday, right in the middle of what I wanted to say, because my eyes were starting to sting and water. That happens when I stare at stuff too long. Dr. Hurst says that'll go away in time. I hope so. It's a pain in the butt. I guess I should write about Dr. Hurst and the hospital and all that stuff, but first I really want to finish writing about that day in the woods because . . . well, because I'm still trying to sort it all out.

When I left off, Megan and Tony had ridden down the trail with Daisy, and I was still up in the tree. I waited there until they had a pretty good head start, so Daisy wouldn't hear me and come bounding back, then I climbed down and started off after them. When they didn't find me anywhere along the trail, I figured they'd probably take Daisy all the way back to my house, which meant they'd have to pass me on their way back to Megan's. As long as Daisy wasn't with them, though, I'd be okay. When I heard them coming, I'd just duck behind a rock or climb another tree.

It was late in the afternoon by then, and the temperature was starting to drop. I was on the eastern side of the mountain, too, where there's no sun in the afternoon. Even though I had a heavy sweatshirt on, I was starting to wish I hadn't left my coat behind. I folded my arms over my chest and tucked my hands under my armpits to keep them warm. The knuckles on my right hand were all skinned and bleeding from smacking the tree, and they stung. I kept trudging along, but to tell the truth, I was starting to get really cold. It would take me a good hour to get home, and even though I was in good shape, my legs were getting tired from slogging along in my heavy boots. I started thinking about that guy who froze to death on Mount Washington and how it would be really embarrassing to freeze to death practically in your own backyard. I *was* practically in my own backyard, too. My house and Megan's are pretty close to each other as the crow flies. It's just that the mountain is in between.

I looked up at the mountain and started to think. I knew I could be home in half the time if I climbed it. And the thing is, I knew I could do it, too. I mean, I'd already climbed Top-o'-the-World, and that was the highest peak on the ridge. I hesitated awhile, remembering the promise I'd made my mother about not climbing again without safety gear, but then I decided what the heck. It was sort of an emergency. I mean, she wouldn't have wanted me to freeze to death, would she?

I looked the cliffs over carefully. They were so steep that there wasn't much snow on them, but there were lots of places where ice had oozed out, dripping down the mountain face like giant stalactites. I didn't think that would be a problem, though. There were still lots of bare places in between. Besides, in addition to saving time, climbing the mountain meant I didn't have to worry about running into Tony and Megan on the lower trail.

That made my mind up. I decided to go for it. I found a route that was pretty much ice-free and started up. It was fun, actually. The truth is, I love danger. It takes my mind off everything else. Once I started up that mountain, all my troubling thoughts were gone. All I had time to worry about was where to put my foot next, where to move my hand.

I could tell right away that it was going to be harder than it had been last time I'd climbed. I'd had sneakers on then. My boots were clumsy, and the thick rubber soles didn't grab very well. But to be honest, I didn't care. I just looked at it as more of a challenge and focused on how great it would feel to get to the top.

The top. I looked up. It was a long way. And my fingers were already cold. I'd started, though. I wasn't about to quit. I never quit something once I start. Don't think, just climb, I told myself. It went pretty well for a while, so well that I started congratulating myself on being "the man" when it came to mountain climbing. I started thinking maybe I'd even enter some competitions, become a pro. But then my fingers started to stiffen and sting, and soon my toes were stinging, too, despite my heavy boots.

Then my foot slipped. God, I'm breaking out in a sweat just remembering it. I was okay, though. I slid a few feet, then grabbed a small root and caught myself. I clung to the mountain for a few minutes, waiting for my heart to stop pounding. I didn't feel much like congratulating myself anymore; in fact, a giant pit had opened up in my stomach.

I started up again, but then I slipped a couple more times. Soon I was sweating all the way through my sweatshirt, and I was beginning to realize that I was in trouble. I thought of giving up, but I was past the midway point by then. It would have taken longer to go back down than to continue up. And then I'd still be an hour from home. I had no choice but to go on.

I inched my way upward, but somehow, the top never seemed to get closer. My hands felt like clumsy claws, and my boots weighed on my legs like anchors. I was sweating and shivering at the same time.

I reached up and tried to feel for the next handhold. My hand found a niche, but I couldn't tell if it was secure. I looked up, and in that instant, a chunk of ice and rock broke free from somewhere higher up. I tried to duck, but it was too late. It hit me square in the face, and I felt a sharp stab of pain in my right eye. I shut it tight and clung to the mountain, waiting for the pain to subside, but it didn't. I tried to blink, tried to rid my eye of the ice and dirt, but I couldn't.

There's no real way to describe the panic I felt. "NO," a voice kept crying out inside me. "NO! This can't be happening. Not again!" I tried to rub my eye with my claw of a hand, but the slightest touch felt like I was slicing across my eyeball with a knife. Fear exploded in my belly then. I was alone, on the side of a mountain, in the freezing cold, with the sun going down.

AND I WAS BLIND.

Tuesday, February 11

Lenny just called. He's having a tough day today, so we talked for a while. He's been coming over a lot since I got out of the hospital, and we've been helping each other through the bad days. He took a leave of absence from school, so he doesn't have to go back until the fall. But that's sort of getting ahead of things again. I need to write about how I got into the hospital before I write about how I got out.

I screamed. Or so they tell me. It's all kind of a blur. I know Megan and Tony found me, and I remember Tony coming down the mountain with a rope and the horses pulling us up. Maybe I blacked out then or something, because the next thing I remember, I was in the hospital. I guess I owe Tony my life, and I'm not sure how I feel about that.

It's scary, being blind. Really scary. That night, in the hospital, I felt the bandages on my face and thought about what it would be like to be blind forever. I'd thought about it before, of course. When you only have one eye, you think about it sometimes. But you never think it will really happen. I didn't anyway. But it did. It did.

My stomach was one big aching knot. I thought about all the things I'd never get to do again if I was blind—like drive, ride my dirt bike, watch TV, play football, go to a movie. Then I thought of all the things I'd never see again—the mountains, the sunset on the ocean, Megan's face, my parents', Kat's, Nick's. Nick was still a kid, still had a baby face. I might never know how he'd look when he was grown.

I wasn't even sure I wanted to live if I was going to be blind. I mean, it would have been one thing if I had been born that way and didn't know what I was missing. Or even if an accident happened that I'd had no control over. That might have been easier to handle somehow. But to know what I was missing, and to know I had done it to myself? I wasn't sure I could live with that.

I remembered what Dr. Thomas had said at my checkup last fall when my mother had told him she couldn't get me to wear the polycarbonate glasses he'd prescribed for me.

"Well, Luke," he'd said in a sad voice. "If you injure your other eye, we'll do everything we can to patch it up. But all I can say is, you're never going to see any better than you see today."

I still get a lump in my throat every time I think about that. How could I have been so dumb? How could I have tempted fate that way? I remember lying in the hospital that night thinking over and over, *This can't be happening. It can't. I'm going to wake up soon and find out it was just a bad dream.*

But it wasn't. It was real.

I felt bitter, too. WHY ME? I mean, what were the odds of something like this happening to someone *twice*? I thought about praying, but it seemed useless. It seemed pretty obvious that God had turned his back on me.

My parents were as scared as I was. My dad kept pacing . . . pacing . . . And every now and then, he would just grab my hand or my knee and squeeze. I could hear my mom sitting over in the corner sniffling. I'd made her cry again. I thought briefly that perhaps it might have been better for my parents if I *had* fallen off the mountain or frozen to death. Now I know that that would have hurt them more than all the rest of the hurts put together.

Crisp footsteps entered the room. A nurse wrapped a blood-pressure cuff around my arm and started pumping.

"Gonna get some more snow?" my father asked.

"God, I hope not," said the nurse. "I've had enough."

My father grunted in agreement.

"U Mass won again last night," the nurse said. "You been following the games?"

"Yeah," my father answered unenthusiastically. "I think they're going all the way."

Hospital small talk. How I hate it. Light, meaningless words to hide the fear.

The nurse ripped the cuff off my arm again and stuck a thermometer in my mouth. "It won't be long now," she said. "There was a little delay, but the O.R.'s all ready and the doctor is on her way."

Delays. There are always delays. The waiting is the hardest part.

"They say she's a good doctor," my mother said. She said it like a statement, but I knew it was really a question.

The nurse pulled the thermometer from my mouth. "Yes," she confirmed. "The best."

I'd have felt better if Dr. Thomas were operating. I knew him. I trusted him. I knew if anyone could save my eye, he could. But Dr. Thomas does retinas, not corneas. Besides, he was back in Boston and I was out here now.

"You want the TV on?" my father asked.

I shrugged and my dad took my indifference for a yes. He switched on the set and I listened to it drone, trying not to think as the time crawled by. At last the nurse came in to give me a shot. It was almost time to go down. The shot made me warm and groggy, took the sharp edge off my fear. Then the orderly came with the stretcher, and my father helped me climb on. The orderly rolled me toward the door, then stopped. Someone bent close and I smelled my mother's perfume. Soft, cool hands cupped my face, and she kissed my forehead. "I love you," she said softly.

I reached my arms around her and hugged her. "I love you, too, Mom," I whispered.

A hand grabbed mine and squeezed. Dad. His grip was fierce and mine equally fierce in return. I didn't want him to let go. "Will you be in the recovery room?" I asked.

"Yes." His voice was shaky. "We'll be there."

Yes. They always are.

Wednesday, February 12

I had my checkup today. I told Dr. Hurst that I'm having a hard time getting used to this contact lens, and she said maybe we should try another kind. She said she'd order it, and it should be in early next week. I wish I had my real lens back, the one that used to be on the inside of my eye. You just don't appreciate how well your body works until something goes wrong with it. My real lens never stung or made my eyes water. I never had to take it out and clean it. It didn't get dust on it and scratch me. It was perfect. And now it's gone. Just like my left eye.

Dr. Hurst says things are going "as well as can be expected." I guess that's how I'm going to see for the rest of my life—"as well as can be expected." At least I can see. I guess I have to be grateful for that.

The morning after the surgery was pretty scary. When Dr. Hurst unwrapped the bandages from my head, bright light stabbed my eyes, making both of them water: the artificial one, and the injured one.

I blinked carefully—there was still a lot of pain—but I could see light and some blurry shapes.

"What can you see?" asked Dr. Hurst.

"Not much," I told her. "It hurts too much to keep them open for long, and everything is blurry."

"That's to be expected," she said. "We put some antibiotic ointment in there, and until we get you fitted for a contact lens, everything will be blurry."

She took her fingers and forced my eyelid open. My

eye jerked with little spasms of pain as she leaned closer. "It looks good," she said. "We cleaned out all the debris, removed the torn lens, and sealed the puncture. How are you feeling otherwise?"

I shrugged. "Okay, I guess. Kind of tired."

"Surgery will do that to you," said Dr. Hurst. "But you're young and healthy. You'll feel like your old self in a few days." She pressed a tissue into my hand, and I dabbed at the tears that oozed out of my eye.

I took a deep breath and worked up the courage to ask the question I was so afraid of. "Will I . . . be able to see okay?"

"Well," said Dr. Hurst, "barring any further complications . . ."

Barring any further complications! Goose bumps prickled my skin. Barring any further complications, I would still have two eyes.

"What kind of complications?" my mother asked.

"Infection is always the main concern with this type of injury," said Dr. Hurst. "But we're going to keep him pumped full of antibiotics, and he should be okay."

"How long before we know exactly how good his vision will be?" my father asked.

"That will take awhile," said Dr. Hurst. "We'll keep the pressure bandage on for a week, then we can fit him for a contact lens."

"Can you . . . give us an idea of what we can hope for?" asked my mother.

Dr. Hurst's voice was kind. "I don't know about you," she said brightly, "but I always hope for the best."

"What about scarring?" my mother asked. "He had a tremendous problem with scarring in the other eye. That's what kept pulling the retina back off."

"Well . . ." There was the slightest hint of hesitation in Dr. Hurst's voice, and for a second my blood turned icy. "I don't anticipate any trouble this time," she went on. "Let's just hope for the best, okay?"

"Okay," my mother said, but I could tell that she, like me, was left wanting—wanting promises, wanting guarantees. But we had learned the hard way that when it came to medicine, there were no guarantees. All there was, was waiting.

"When can I go home?" I asked quietly.

"If you still had your other eye," said Dr. Hurst, "I'd let you go home tomorrow, but under the circumstances, we're going to keep you right here and baby you for a while."

"What?" I said. "How long a while?"

"Oh, at least a week."

"A week!" I turned toward my parents. "C'mon, you're not gonna let her keep me here a week!"

"Oh, not here," said Dr. Hurst. "We need this bed for the *sick* patients. We're going to move you down to another wing where you'll be with some people your own age."

"I don't want to be with anybody, my own age or not," I said. "I just want to go home. My parents can take care of me. They've had lots of experience."

Dr. Hurst's blurry shape loomed close again. "I can't take that chance, Luke," she said. "This eye is too important to me. It should be to you, too."

I thought about that for a long moment, then I sighed and nodded.

"Good," she said, patting my knee. "Now say good-bye to the world of light and color for a while. I've got to put your pressure bandage back on."

I sat quietly while she repacked the shield and wound the bandages around my head again. It all felt so familiar, so horribly, horribly familiar.

"I'll have the auxiliary send up some books on tape," she said. "Anything else you need?"

"You got any Beetle Wings?" I asked.

"Beetle Wings?" There was a question in Dr. Hurst's voice. "What on earth is a Beetle Wing?"

My parents laughed. "It's an alternative rock group," my mother said.

"Oh." Dr. Hurst laughed, too. "I admit I'm out of touch. I'm not sure the auxiliary has any Beetle Wings, but I can check."

"Don't worry about it," my dad said. "We'll bring his own tapes in."

"Okay," said Dr. Hurst. She tapped my knee again. "I'll check in on you tomorrow."

"Doc?" I said as I heard her footsteps retreating.

"Yes?"

"Thanks . . ."—my voice broke and I had to clear my throat—"for everything."

"My pleasure," said Dr. Hurst quietly. "Just promise that once we get you patched up, you're going to wear those polycarbonate lenses."

"I promise," I said softly.

Once she was gone, my parents' footsteps closed in on the bed. My mother's cool hand stroked my brow.

Suddenly something dawned on me. "Wrestling!" I cried, sitting up in bed. "What about the meet this weekend?"

"Sorry, Luke," my dad said gently. "Wrestling's over for you for this year."

"Over?" I cried. "What do you mean, over?"

"I mean Dr. Hurst says no sports until at least the summer."

I swallowed hard and sank back against the pillow. "That stinks," I said quietly. Then I got angry, really angry—at myself. I'd let everybody down again: my parents, my coach, the team. . . . I squeezed my hand into a fist and banged it down beside me on the bed. "I'm such a jerk," I said through clenched teeth. "When am I going to stop being such a jerk?"

There was a silence, and then my father cleared his throat. "Luke," he said, "there's another matter we need to talk about."

"What?" I asked.

"They're going to move you to another floor soon, and a new doctor will be coming in to talk to you."

"I don't want a new doctor," I said. "I like Dr. Hurst."

"Oh, you'll still have Dr. Hurst," my father said. "This is another kind of doctor."

"What other kind of doctor?"

There was a moment's hesitation, and then my mother said, "A psychologist."

Her words shocked me. "A what? A shrink! What for?"

Someone's hand touched mine, but I pushed it away. "What's going on?" I said. "You guys think I'm crazy now?"

"Of course not, Luke," said my father.

"Well, what then? What do I need a shrink for?"

My father cleared his throat once more. "We're worried, Luke," he said. "We don't understand . . . why you do the things you do."

"We're afraid, Luke," my mother said quietly. "Afraid of losing you."

"You're *not* going to lose me," I said impatiently. "Believe me, I've learned my lesson this time."

There was a long silence, then, in a broken voice, my mother said, "Do you know how many times we've heard that, Luke?"

A jagged lump formed in my throat, and I clenched my jaws to fight back the tears. Someone touched my hand again. This time, I didn't pull away.

"We can't go on like this," my father said, "wondering and worrying every time you're out of sight, living in fear of what the next hour might bring. . . ."

I didn't answer.

"We love you so much, Luke," my mother said. "You know we do. Please try to understand."

I sighed and nodded tiredly.

"You'll be home soon," my mother said. "You'll see. Megan keeps calling, by the way. She and Tony would like to come in and see you."

I squeezed my eyes tight. "I don't want to see anybody," I said through clenched teeth, "and I don't want anybody to ever know . . . about the shrink."

Thursday, February 13

I had my session with Jim today. He's the shrink. He's been testing me for learning disabilities and something called ADD, which he says can contribute to problems like mine. I still see him a couple times a week. He's not bad, actually—not as bad as I thought he was going to be. He's not old or scary, and he doesn't yell or talk with an accent you can't understand like some of the shrinks in the movies.

I really didn't know what to expect that day in the hospital when they wheeled me down to the psych ward. I remember lying in my new bed wondering where I was, and what the place looked like, and if my roommate was going to be some kind of psycho lunatic. And then I remembered something that really gave me the shivers. *Holden Caulfield.* Man, that was creepy. I'd ended up like him after all. I mean, not that I was really in a mental institution. But I was in a psychiatric ward. Pretty much the same thing, I guessed.

Crazy! I couldn't get over the fact that they thought I was crazy. I was even starting to worry that maybe I was. I didn't know what to think anymore. Then there was this sudden knock on the door, and I nearly jumped out of my skin.

"What?" I said, turning toward the sound.

"May I come in?" a man's voice asked. It sounded like a pretty normal voice, so I relaxed a little bit.

"I guess so," I said.

Footsteps approached the bed. "I'm Dr. Spellman," the man said cheerfully, "but most of my patients call me Jim."

"You the shrink?" I asked.

Dr. Spellman laughed. "I prefer 'pediatric psychologist,'" he said, "but I've been known to answer to almost anything."

"I don't think I need a shrink," I said.

"Maybe not," said Dr. Spellman, "but the nice thing about a psychological evaluation is that it doesn't hurt. There are no needles, no enemas, no cutting or scraping. We don't even have to starve you. So what have you got to lose?"

"What have I got to lose?" I repeated. "Suppose you give me this evaluation and decide I *am* crazy. What then—lock me up and throw away the key?"

"Of course not, Luke," said Dr. Spellman. "Nobody thinks you're crazy."

"Yeah, right," I snapped. "I know how these places are. You guys love messing with people's heads. If they're not crazy when they come in, you make them crazy in no time."

"You've been watching too many movies, Luke," Dr. Spellman said quietly. "We *don't* think you're crazy, and we don't have any ulterior motives. We just think you might be a little troubled, that's all, and if we can get at what's troubling you, then maybe we can help you live a happier life."

"I *am* happy," I told him.

"Are you?"

"Sure."

"Happy on the outside, or all the way clean clear through?"

I thought for a moment about the inside of me, the all the way deep *down* inside. I touched my hand, fingered the scabs on my scraped knuckles. "Give me a break," I said quietly. "Who's happy all the way clean clear through?"

Dr. Spellman told me that my sessions would start the next day and then went out and left me alone again. More waiting. If I *was* crazy, I wanted to find out about it quick instead of having to wait and wonder. Then more footsteps entered the room.

"Hi," someone said. It was a young man's voice this time. An oddly familiar young man's voice.

"Hi," I said cautiously.

"I'm your roommate," the guy told me. Then, "Hey, you look familiar."

I felt my body tensing. That was the last thing I wanted, someone I knew seeing me there.

"Luke? Is that you under those bandages? It's me. Lenny."

Lenny! Goose bumps stood up on my arms.

"Luke?"

"Y-Yeah," I said haltingly. "It's me. How—how are you doing, Lenny?"

"I'm okay." There was an awkward silence. "But . . . what are *you* doing here?"

"I . . . uh, hurt my eye," I said.

"The blind one?" Lenny asked.

"No," I told him. "The good one."

"Wow." Lenny's voice filled with concern. "That's tough. Is it gonna be okay?"

"Yeah. They think so."

"That's good. Jeez. It'd be awful if anything happened to your other eye, huh?"

"Yeah," I said quietly.

"Especially the way you wrestle and all."

"What do you mean?" I asked him.

"Jeez, you're a legend," he said, "the way you wrestle with only one eye, wearing that mask and all. I met a couple of guys up at State who used to be on some of the teams we wrestled last year. You know what they call you?"

I shrugged.

"Cyclops," said Lenny.

I smiled. "No kidding?"

"No kidding."

There was a short silence, then Lenny cleared his throat. "I . . . uh, hope I wasn't out of line, telling you that," he said. "About the guys calling you Cyclops, I mean. I hope you don't take offense. . . ."

I shook my head. "Naw," I said. "I think it's kind of cool." Then my smile faded. Lot of good any of that did me, or my team, now.

"You sure your eye's gonna be okay?" Lenny asked again.

"Yeah," I said, as much to convince myself as to convince him. "I think so."

"That's good. Man, that must've been scary. How long do you have to wear the bandage?"

"Another week or so."

"How'd it happen?"

"Long story," I said.

"So why'd they put you down here?" Lenny asked.

My throat tightened. "They . . . uh, needed the bed upstairs for somebody sicker."

"Oh."

Lenny didn't buy it, I could tell, but he didn't push me any further.

"Hungry?" he asked. "I've got all kinds of junk food."

"No," I said a bit too harshly. I was worn out with talking. "I'm just . . . tired, okay?"

"Oh sure, I understand," said Lenny. "Go ahead, get some rest. We got lots of time. We'll talk later, okay?"

"Sure," I said. "Later."

Friday, February 14

I just had another argument with my mother. The phone rang while she was up here changing my sheets, and she answered it. It was Megan, and even though I've told her a million times I don't want to talk to Megan, she tried to hand me the phone.

"No," I whispered. "Tell her I'm sleeping."

My mother made an exasperated face and put her hand over the mouthpiece.

"I've been telling her that for weeks," she said, "and it's getting to be embarrassing. She knows you're not sleeping. Why don't you just talk to her?"

"I don't want to."

"Come on. It's Valentine's Day."

"I don't care. I *don't* want to talk to her."

"Why not? She's a nice girl."

"I just don't, okay?" I said. "Now mind your own business and leave me alone."

My mother sighed deeply, then took back the phone. "He doesn't want to talk to you," she said, then she hung up.

I couldn't believe it! "What did you do that for?" I shouted. "That was downright rude."

"No," said my mother. "You're the one who's being downright rude, and I think you ought to think about the way you're treating that girl." Then she stalked out of the room.

· · ·

The way I'm treating that girl? What about the way she treated me, huh? Doesn't that count? I swear, if I am crazy, my parents are half the reason. I had a big fight with my dad the other night, too. He came up to say good night, and he asked me if I'd done the homework Hutch had dropped off. Well, I hadn't, of course, and of course he wanted to know why.

"Because I've been busy," I said.

"Busy doing what?" I asked.

"Writing in my journal. It's an English assignment."

"Well, that's good," he said, "but I don't want you to neglect your other work."

For some reason, it made me really mad when he said that. Probably because (a) he hounds me about homework all the time, and (b) I *was* neglecting my other work and didn't want to be reminded of it.

"You don't want to fall behind," my dad went on. "This is a critical year . . ."

". . . a critical year for getting into college," I finished sarcastically.

My dad frowned. "Well, it is, Luke. And at the rate you're going, you'll never get . . ."

". . . never get into a school like Kat got into?" I snapped. "Well, maybe I don't want to go to a school like Kat got into. Maybe I don't want to go to college at all. Why don't you just get off my back!"

My dad stood staring at me for a long time, then he sighed a deep, tired sigh.

"Okay, Luke," he said. "Have it your way. If you don't want your mother and me to worry about you anymore, we won't, okay? You do your own thing from now on. You come and go as you please. Study when you want, don't study when you want. And if you don't want to go to college, that's your choice, too. Have a good life."

Then he walked out. And I felt like crap. Because the thing is, I'd like a little more freedom, but to be honest, I don't think I'm ready for *that* much. I mean, to tell the truth, I *am* a procrastinator, and I do sort of depend on my parents to kick my butt now and then. And to be honest, I really do want to go to college, and I'd even be kind of proud to go to a really good one. It's just that I don't want my parents to know that because then, if I didn't get in, they might be disappointed. It's complicated—this whole parents thing.

My parents came to one of the sessions with Jim, the first one, in fact. But it didn't help much. I was still pretty mad about everything that day—about getting hurt again and my parents thinking I needed a shrink. And I felt snuck up on, too, because I didn't know my parents were coming until they actually walked in.

"I usually like to start out talking with the family together," Jim said, "so I've invited your parents in for the first half hour of this session. Is that okay with you, Luke?"

No, it wasn't okay, but what did he expect me to say with them standing there? I just shrugged and said, "Whatever."

My parents came over and sat down on either side of me. Talk about feeling surrounded! The tension between us was thick enough to cut. I didn't want to be there. I didn't think I belonged there. I was a perfectly normal kid whose parents thought he was crazy.

"So, Luke, I hear you're quite a wrestler," Jim said, an attempt, obviously, at breaking the ice. "How's the season going?"

"It's over," I snapped.

"Already?"

"I, uh, think he means it's over for him," my father put in. "Dr. Hurst won't allow him to wrestle anymore this season."

I turned toward my father's voice. "I don't need an interpreter," I growled.

"Is that what you meant, Luke?" asked Jim.

"Yes," I snapped.

"I'm sorry to hear that," Jim went on. "That must be a big disappointment for you."

I didn't answer.

"Would you like to talk about it?" Jim asked.

"I don't feel like talking about anything," I said.

"All right," said Jim, "then why don't we let your parents talk first? Mr. and Mrs. Carver, why don't you tell me why the family is here today?"

There was a short silence, and then my mother began to speak quietly. "My husband and I are . . . concerned about Luke," she said. "He tends to make some bad choices from time to time. He seems to be making a lot of them lately."

"Not that he's a bad kid," my father jumped in.

"No," my mother quickly agreed. "No. He's a wonderful kid." Her voice grew softer. "The problem is, I don't think he believes that, which is sad, because he has so much to offer."

I sighed. I'd heard how much I "had to offer" so many times, I wanted to puke. My parents give me that same song and dance every time I get into trouble. "You're such a great kid, Luke." "You have so much to offer, Luke." Sometimes I don't think it's me they're talking about at all. I think they've made up some fantasy kid in their heads. I listened to them talk about all my great qualities for a few more minutes, and then I couldn't stand it anymore.

"If I'm so *wonderful*," I growled, "then why am I here?"

Jim chuckled. "Why don't you tell me about some of Luke's bad choices, Mrs. Carver," he said.

"Well . . ."—my mother sighed like she had the weight of the world on her shoulders—"there was a boating incident that nearly resulted in him and a friend being run over by a barge."

"That was *last* summer," I reminded her.

"We've caught him drinking a number of times," said my father. "He went up to a fraternity party at State just last—"

"I didn't even *drink* that night!" I cut in. "I haven't had a drink since last summer."

"There have been several car accidents," my father continued, "some speeding tickets . . ."

"Those *weren't* all my fault," I insisted.

"A hit-and-run accident," my mother added quietly.

"All right!" I shouted. "Enough. Okay? You're making it all sound way worse than it is. Most of that stuff is ancient history."

"Most of it happened within the last year, Luke," my father said softly.

"Yeah? Well, a year is a long time. Besides, you guys overreact to everything."

There was a long silence, and then my mother said, "That's true. We do overreact sometimes, and we probably don't give Luke the kind of freedom a boy his age deserves. But . . . we're just so scared . . ."

I stood up. "Yeah, well maybe that's the problem, Mom," I said. "Maybe you've got to stop being scared and let me live my life, okay?"

"Mrs. Carver," Jim said gently, "why don't you tell Luke what you're afraid of. What is your worst fear for him?"

There was another silence, and then my mother answered haltingly.

"I'm afraid that he's going to end up dead, or in jail."

I turned toward Jim's voice.

"Do you see?" I said. "Do you see what I mean? Jeez."

"You don't think your parents' fears are justified?" Jim asked.

I shook my head. "No," I said. "I think they want to put me in a glass box and keep me on a shelf like a doll."

"No, we don't–" my dad started to say.

"Yes, you do," I interrupted. "Do you know how many times a day you tell me to be careful? Do you realize that you give me the third degree every time I want to go anywhere, do anything?"

"We just want you to be safe," my mother said.

I turned toward her. "Safe?" I said. "And how do I stay safe? By sitting at home and watching movies with you and Dad? That's what you want, isn't it? You want me to stay right where you can see me every minute."

"That's not true," my mother said.

"It *is* true," I said. "Be honest."

There was no answer.

"I don't want to be *safe*," I said quietly. "I don't want to sit home and watch movies about other people living. *I* want to live. *I* want to have fun. When's the last time *you* had fun, Mom–the last time you really felt the thrill of being alive?"

There was another long silence, and then Jim spoke up again.

"Our first half hour is up," he said. "Would you like your parents to stay longer, Luke?"

"No," I said.

They left then, silently, sadly, and I felt bad for making them go. But not bad enough to ask them to stay.

"Well," said Jim after they'd left. "Would you like to talk about what just happened here?"

"No," I said. "I would not."

"All right, then, what would you like to talk about?"

"Nothing," I said. "I'm tired."

"I can sympathize with that," said Jim. "But I'd like to talk a little longer if we could. Why don't you just tell me how you came to hurt your eye?"

"Why don't you read the chart," I said.

Jim chuckled. "I don't mean this eye," he said. "I mean the other one."

I stiffened and the hairs on my body stood up like ruffled feathers. "What's that got to do with anything?" I snapped.

"I don't know. Do you think it has to do with any-thing?"

I frowned. "Is this where you do your shrink thing and keep turning all my questions around and asking them back to me?"

Jim laughed. "No," he said, "not if you don't want me to."

"I don't."

"Okay, fine. I don't know if your old eye injury has anything to do with your present problems or not, Luke. But I'd like to try to find out."

"What problems?" I said. "I don't think I have any problems."

"If that's true," Jim asked softly, "then why do you think your parents are so concerned about you?"

"My parents worry too much," I told him. "They even admitted it. You heard them. They exaggerate everything all out of proportion. I've had a few little accidents. That's all."

"A few?"

My jaw tightened. "Yeah, a few."

"All right," said Jim. "A few. But suffice it to say that several of these 'accidents' have been life-threatening, you've lost one eye and injured the other, and you were the perpetrator of a hit-and-run automobile accident. If you were a parent and these things were happening to your child, don't you think you'd be concerned?"

I shrugged.

"What if they were happening to your younger brother?" asked Jim. "Would you be concerned for him?"

I said nothing.

"Can you understand your mother's fears?" he continued.

"You mean . . . about me dying or going to jail?"

"Yes."

I ground my teeth together and stared into the unending blackness, replaying the conversation with my parents inside my head, listening over and over to my mother's anxious, halting words. Slowly my ruffled feathers smoothed down again.

"I guess so," I said quietly.

"Good," said Jim. "Then let's try to get to the root of what's bothering you, okay?"

I sucked in a deep breath and let it out slowly. "Sure," I said, "whatever."

"All right then. Can we talk about how you hurt your eye?"

I didn't answer, and after an extended silence, Jim sighed. "Luke," he said, "I'm not the enemy. I'm here to help you. And you may find that I'm really not a bad guy if you'll give me a chance. Ask around if you'd like."

Again, I didn't answer right away. I still didn't like the idea of talking to a shrink, but the guy did sound sincere, like he really cared what happened to me, though I didn't know why he should.

"All right, Doc," I said at last. "What do you want from me?"

"Well," said Jim, "for starters, could you call me Jim? Doc sounds so . . . medicinal, and I'm not one of those white-coat-and-tie kinds of doctors. I know you can't see me, but I'm sitting here in my flannel shirt and jeans."

For some reason, that did make me relax a little. "Okay," I said. "Jim it is."

"Good," he said, sounding genuinely pleased. "Now, can we talk about your eye?"

"I guess so," I said warily. "But I still don't see what it's got to do with anything. It happened four years ago, down at our summer place on the Cape. I was wrestling with some friends, and I got poked in the eye with an elbow."

"Really?" said Jim. "That's odd, isn't it?"

My feathers puffed out again instantly. "What do you mean?" I asked.

"Well," said Jim. "It's just that it says here that you sustained a torn retina. It usually takes quite a forceful blow to cause that type of injury."

I was starting to feel cornered again. "So?" I said.

"So . . . it just seems surprising that an elbow could cause that kind of damage. Didn't your eye surgeon think it unusual?" Jim persisted.

"Yes, he thought it was very unusual," I said. "But unusual things happen, you know? Especially to me. Now, can I go? I'm really tired."

"Sure." I heard Jim's pen scribbling again. "Our time's about up anyway. Just one more question, though. Do you have any idea why so many unusual things happen to you?"

"Yeah," I snarled. "God hates me."

Sunday, February 16

I saw Lenny in church this morning with his folks. He looks good—he's put on a little more weight, and has some color back in his cheeks. He still looks really sad, though. I met him outside afterward and asked him if he wanted to come over for a couple of hours, but he said he couldn't. He had to go somewhere with his folks.

"Did you tell them yet?" I asked.

He shook his head and looked down. Just then my parents came along.

"So, give me a call," I said to Lenny in a fake happy voice. "We'll do something during the week."

"Sounds good," he said. But he didn't really sound like anything sounded good to him.

I worry about Lenny a lot. We got to be pretty close in the hospital after I got over lying to him about why I was there. I got caught in that pretty quick. When I got back from my first session with Jim and Lenny asked me where I'd been, I tried to tell him they'd taken me for X rays.

"X rays?" he said.

"Yeah." I showed him my scraped-up hand. "I hurt my hand, too. They wanted to see if anything was broken."

"And they waited this long?"

"Yeah. Well, I forgot to mention it before. I mean, my eye was the big thing, you know?"

"Yeah," said Lenny. "I suppose. Is your hand okay?"

"Yeah, it's fine."

I lay my head back then and pretended I was going to sleep so I wouldn't have to answer any more questions. That's one good thing about having your eyes bandaged: it's real easy to pretend you're asleep.

A short while later footsteps entered the room, and next thing I know, I heard Jim Spellman saying, "You left your Walkman in my office, Luke. Thought you might be looking for it."

Bang. Dead in the water. I didn't know what to say or do, so I decided to just go on pretending I was asleep.

"I'm looking forward to our talk tomorrow," Jim went on. "That was a very interesting note we left off on."

I clenched my teeth together but said nothing. After a moment of silence, I heard Jim place my Walkman on my bedside table.

"How's it going, Lenny?" I heard him ask.

"Fine, Jim."

"Glad to hear it. See you tomorrow."

Jim left and silence filled the room.

"I know you're not sleeping," said Lenny. "Jim knew it, too."

I swallowed hard and rubbed the scabs on my knuckles.

"It's nothing to be ashamed of, you know," Lenny said quietly.

"What?"

"Therapy," said Lenny, "having problems. Everybody in the world has *some* kind of problem."

"Exactly," I said angrily. "And mine are no worse than anybody else's, so why am I here?"

"I don't know," said Lenny. "Why do *you* think you're here?"

If my eyes hadn't been so messed up, I would have rolled them. "You've been hanging with these shrinks too long, Lenny," I said. "You're starting to sound like one of them."

Lenny laughed. "Seriously," he said, "what are you in here for?"

"I told you. *Nothing!*" I snapped. "What are *you* in here for?"

There was a silence, then, in a low, troubled voice, Lenny said, "I tried to kill myself. Didn't you hear?"

I swallowed again. I'd never expected him to come right out and say it.

"Jeez," I said softly. "Why'd you wanna do that, man?"

Lenny sighed heavily. "I don't know. Just depressed, I guess."

"Depressed about what? You got it tough at home or something?"

"No." Lenny's voice sounded very sad. "I've got it great at home. That's half the problem. I think my parents love me *too* much."

I was startled by that. I lay there silently for a while, thinking. "You know," I said at last, "I think maybe I have that same problem."

"Honest?" Lenny's voice perked up. "How do you mean?"

"I don't know," I told him. "It's kind of like my parents got this idea somewhere along the line that I was a great kid, you know? I don't really know where they got it, because it seems to me I've been messing up ever since I was little. But no matter how bad I mess up, they keep telling me how great I am, and how much I have to offer the world, and all that stuff. And so I *try* to be the kid they seem to think I am, but I always end up letting them down somehow, and . . . inside I kind of think that maybe I'm really *not* who they think I am at all, and maybe one of these days they're gonna figure that out and be . . . well . . . I don't know . . . disappointed or something."

There was such a long silence that I wondered if Lenny had walked out of the room while I was talking.

"Lenny?" I said. "You still there?"

"Yeah." Lenny's voice was soft and husky. I think maybe he'd been crying.

Tuesday, February 18

My new lens came in today, and I went in to get it fitted. It seems pretty good so far. I can see the best yet, and my eyes haven't watered at all. Dr. Hurst is going to check it again on Friday, and if it's still doing okay, she says I can start back to school on Monday.

I'm not sure I'm too happy about that. Not that I love sitting around here all day, but it's going to be weird seeing people again. I'm sure I'm the talk of the school. I don't know what's going to be worse—all the kids staring at me, or all the teachers trying to pretend like nothing happened so I don't feel bad.

I wonder what Megan thinks of me now. Does *she* think I'm crazy? I really miss her a lot, but I'm afraid to see her. I don't know why. Maybe I should talk to Jim about it tomorrow. I kind of like to plan ahead what I'm going to talk to Jim about anyway; otherwise, he starts bringing things up on his own. And that can get a little hairy, because he latches onto things sometimes. It's like he smells blood, and he just keeps on the trail until he corners you and there's no escape. Like that time I told him that God hated me—he brought that up every day after that until it was all I could think about. I just kept going over in my head all the times God had spanked me, all the times he'd whacked me upside the head for doing little things that everyone else seemed to get away with. The more I thought about it, the more unfair it seemed, until one day, when Jim brought it up, I just blurted everything out.

"You really think God hates you?" Jim asked.

"Yeah," I said. "I really do."

"Why, Luke?"

"Because He spanks me every time I turn around. Look at me. How do you think I ended up in here?"

"I'm not sure," said Jim. "Would you like to fill me in on the details?"

"I went mountain climbing. Big deal."

"I see. Are you a mountain climber?"

"Yeah. Well, sort of."

"So you've had a lot of experience?" he said.

"No. Well, yeah. But not officially. I just joined the out-doors club in school." I began to feel antsy, wondering what Jim was sniffing out this time.

"And was this a club climb?"

"No. It was just me."

I could hear Jim's pen scratching. What was he writing? I wondered. What was he saying about me? I was starting to feel hunted, and I needed to move. I stood up and started pacing, which isn't easy to do when you're blind. I tripped on the rug and bumped into the desk.

"What are you trying to do, Luke?" Jim asked.

"I gotta move," I said, running my hand through my hair. "I hate sitting still."

"I see. Okay. Well, let me clear a path for you here. There, you should be able to move now if you want."

"Thanks," I said, pacing a little more carefully.

"So, where were we?" said Jim. "Oh yes, you took your gear and went for a climb–"

"I didn't say anything about gear," I snapped. I could

tell Jim was laying down some sort of trap, and my feathers were ruffling up again.

There was a silence.

"You didn't take any gear?"

"No."

"Was this just a small climb?"

"It was West Mountain, east face."

Jim gasped. "All the way to the top?"

"That's the idea of climbing a mountain, isn't it?" I said.

"Yes," said Jim. "But . . . that's quite a climb."

I slowed my pacing. "Yeah," I said. "Well, I never made it to the top anyway. That's where the accident happened, with my eye. About three-quarters of the way up."

Jim let out a low whistle. "So you were stuck, . . . three-quarters of the way up the east face of West Mountain, totally blind?"

"That's right." My stomach knotted up, remembering.

"How did you get off?"

"My friends came along. They found my jacket and came looking for me—"

"You didn't have your jacket on?" Jim interrupted.

"No. I didn't have my jacket on," I barked. "What's that got to do with anything?"

"Did you have gloves on at least?"

"No."

"Hiking boots?"

"No."

"I see."

There was another silence, and I got the sense I'd

somehow been backed into some kind of corner again.

"You *see*?" I shouted. "What do you see? Because I can't see a freakin' thing!"

"You seem to blame God for some of these things that have happened to you," said Jim. "Do you feel that God gets you into these situations?

"No," I said through clenched teeth.

"Then who does?"

I threw my hands up in frustration. "I do, I guess."

"And who gets you out?" asked Jim.

"I don't know," I snapped. "I don't care. I just want to go back to my room, okay?"

I heard Jim rise from his chair and walk across the room. What was he doing, I wondered? Moving to his desk? Looking out the window? Or was he circling, closing in for the kill? I started pacing again.

"So, if you don't blame God for the situations you've gotten into," he said, "what exactly do you blame Him for?"

"Punishing me," I shouted. "Punishing me for nothing, all the time."

"I see," said Jim, "and you take these punishments as a sign of God's hatred?"

"Wouldn't you?" I asked.

"Not necessarily," said Jim.

I stopped pacing and turned in the direction of his voice.

"I get a lot of troubled kids in here, Luke," Jim went on. "Lots of them complain to me about how tough their parents are on them, about the punishments they receive when they get into trouble. Those aren't the kids I worry about. I worry about the kids nobody punishes. Do you know why?"

Chills prickled in the roots of my hair. "Why?" I said quietly.

"Because those are the kids nobody cares about," he said. I heard him moving toward me, then I felt a hand on my shoulder. "If God *is* spanking you," he said, "then I'd say you must be someone He really cares about."

I thought about that for a moment, and it made sense at first, made me feel a little better about God and me, but then, the more I thought about it, the more I felt the old anger again.

"You think so?" I said bitterly. Then I tapped the bandage over my artificial eye. "Kind of a tough punishment for a thirteen-year-old kid, don't you think?"

There was silence for a while, and then Jim said, "Are you angry with God, Luke?"

Tears stung my eyes for a second, but I fought them back.

"Because it's okay if you are," said Jim. "God's ways are hard to understand sometimes."

I bit my lip and shrugged. "I just wish he'd quit spanking me," I said.

"I don't think God's spanking you, Luke," said Jim. "I think you're spanking yourself."

I jerked Jim's hand off my shoulder. "Spanking myself?" I said. "What's that supposed to mean?"

"It means," said Jim calmly, "that either consciously or subconsciously you're making choices that put you at risk."

"At risk for what?"

"Danger, or punishment, or both."

I frowned. "And *why* would I want to do that?"

"I don't know. Why don't you tell me?"

I sighed in exasperation and leaned my head back. The whole conversation was exhausting.

"I don't know," I said softly. "I don't know."

"Do you like yourself, Luke?" Jim asked.

I swallowed down the lump that had formed in my throat, glad, for once, for the bandage around my head. Glad I didn't have to worry about the tears that suddenly sprang to my eyes.

"Luke?"

"I don't know," I said quietly.

"Do you want to talk about it?"

"No."

"Are you sure?"

"Yes, I'm sure."

"Okay. Go back to your room and get some rest, then. We'll talk more next time."

I was wiped out when I got back to my room that night. Those sessions can really drain everything right out of you.

"You look beat," Lenny said. "How'd it go?"

I let out a sigh. "This stuff is more tiring than wrestling practice," I said.

"Yeah," said Lenny. "That's for sure."

"Do you think they're helping you any?" I asked him. "I mean, are you less depressed than when you came here?"

Lenny sighed. "I don't know. I guess I'm doing better. They put me on some medicine, and they took me off suicide watch. I'm not sure how it's gonna be when I go back home, though."

I thought about going back home, back to Daisy, and Nick and Kat, and my parents, back to my dirt bike and riding in the woods. I thought of how lucky I was and how happy I should be to go back, but Jim's question was still sitting in my gut like a lump of rotten meat. *"Do you like yourself, Luke?"*

No. I didn't like myself. And I was afraid that if my parents knew the real me, they wouldn't like me either.

"When I think about the other kids in here, I think I really *must* be nuts," Lenny went on. "I mean, a lot of them are in here because they've got parents that have beaten them, raped them, abandoned them, you name it. And here I am complaining because my parents love me too much."

I nodded slowly. "Yeah. It sounds kind of crazy. But it's not. What's your family like, Lenny? I don't know anything about them."

"My parents are older," Lenny told me. "I was kind of a surprise. They had my three sisters first and weren't planning on any more kids. Then I came along. My mom has always called me her 'bonus baby.'"

There was a lot of warmth and love in Lenny's voice as he talked, but there was an undercurrent of sadness, too.

He laughed a little. "I guess I must've been the most spoiled rotten baby in the world," he said. "My mom and my big sisters did nothing but fuss over me, and my dad . . ."

Lenny's voice broke, and he had to clear his throat before he could go on. "My dad was so thrilled to have a son. He did everything with me: fishing, camping, baseball games . . . everything."

"Sounds like a great life," I said.

"Yeah." Lenny's voice was husky. "I just wish I could be . . . everything they want me to be."

I nodded. "Me, too," I said quietly. "Have you told them how you feel?"

"No. Have you told yours?"

My stomach squeezed into a knot. "No . . . I haven't told them."

"See, that's the thing . . ." Lenny's voice was starting to quiver. "I don't . . . I don't think I *can* tell them."

I turned toward his voice. "Well, what is it that you can't tell them?" I asked. "Did something really bad happen? Are you flunking out of school or something?"

"No." Lenny's voice was real trembly now. "It's way worse than that."

I tried to think of worse things than flunking out. "Did you . . . get some girl in trouble?" I asked.

"No."

"You into drugs?"

"No." There was a small sob. This guy was really hurting.

"What then?" I said. "What could be so bad?"

There was another sob, and then Lenny said, "I'm gay."

The hair on my head prickled and my breath caught in my throat. I didn't know what to say. At first I thought maybe Lenny was kidding, pulling my leg. I mean, he's about the furthest thing from a gay-looking guy that *I've* ever seen. He's almost as big as me, and his voice is a regular guy voice. He's even got hair on his chest!

But then, he didn't sound like he was kidding, sitting over there sobbing like that.

"See?" he said. "Even you're disgusted."

To be honest, the whole thing *was* sort of giving me the creeps. Not that I'm one of those homophobics or anything, but . . . I mean, I was up close and personal with this guy's butt all last year during wrestling practice!

Lenny tried to stifle another sob, and I knew I had to say something.

"No . . . ," I said haltingly. "I'm . . . not disgusted. I'm just . . . I don't know what to say, man. I mean, are you sure? How do you know?"

Lenny gave a short laugh. "I *know*, okay?" he said. "I just know."

I got that creepy feeling again. "Have you . . . actually been with a guy?" I asked.

"No," said Lenny. "I've never been with a guy, or a girl either."

"Then how can you be sure?" I questioned. "Maybe . . ."

"Luke"–Lenny's voice quavered–"I'm sure. Believe me. This is the last thing I'd ever want. I've tried to deny it, but I can't anymore. It's just too strong."

I guess I really blew it at that point. I knew what Lenny needed. He needed me to comfort him, to tell him it wasn't so bad. But I couldn't bring myself to do it. The truth was, a part of me really *was* disgusted. I mean, he was telling me he liked guys, and I was a guy, and–I'm ashamed to say it now–I was starting to wonder if he was over there giving me the eye, and it kind of made my skin crawl.

The silence stretched out and got pretty uncomfortable. Then there was this heavy sigh and Lenny said, "Don't worry, Luke. You're not my type."

I should've said something right then and there, I guess, but I didn't. Some friend, huh?

Wednesday, February 19

I talked to Jim about Megan at my session today. He said I need to be honest with her, to tell her why I broke up with her. These shrinks are very big on honesty. Easier said than done, I say.

I mean, suppose I go over there and tell her I broke up with her because I was afraid we were getting too serious, and suppose she laughs and says she wasn't serious at all? Besides, what's the point? Even if she did really care about me once, she probably thinks I'm a nut case now. The only friend I'm really sure of anymore is Lenny. And that's only because he's a nut case, too.

That wasn't fair. I shouldn't have said that. I was just feeling sorry for myself. Lenny's not a nut case at all. He's just got an awful lot on his mind. Even more than me.

I still feel bad about the way I reacted that night when Lenny told me he was gay. I really hurt his feelings, and he didn't talk much for a couple of days after, which was good, actually, because it gave me time to think, and I finally realized I was being a jerk. I mean, it wasn't as if Lenny *became* gay overnight and suddenly I didn't like him. He'd been gay all along, and I'd always liked him before I knew, so why should knowing change anything?

I started thinking about how tough it must be for him. I mean, like he said, he didn't *want* to be gay. It's just what he is. Every now and then I come up against someone who seems to have a problem with the way my false eye looks.

It bothers some people that the lid droops a little and the eye doesn't track quite right, and they kind of shy away from me, even though it's something I have no control over and has nothing to do with who I am inside. And that hurts. But I can usually handle it. I just figure those people aren't worth knowing anyway. But it must be tough for Lenny to tell himself that, knowing that most of the freakin' world would want to shy away from him.

Anyway, I finally got up the nerve to apologize to him one afternoon, but it was pretty quiet over on his side of the room, and I wasn't sure if he was sleeping.

"Hey, Lenny," I whispered.

There was a heavy sigh but no answer.

"Lenny," I said. "You okay?"

I heard the sheets swishing around, and another sigh, but still no answer. I thought about the way he'd been so quiet the past couple of days, and I started to worry that maybe I'd made him depressed all over again, that maybe I'd wrecked everything the doctors had been trying to fix. I slipped quietly out of my bed and groped my way toward his. The privacy curtain was pulled over, and when I yanked it back, I heard Lenny gasp.

"Lenny?" I said, groping along the bed. I found his arm and grabbed it. "What's up, man? You okay?"

"Huh? What?"

He sounded funny, dazed sort of.

"Lenny," I said, shaking his arm. "What's wrong?"

"Nothing," he said. "What's wrong with you?"

"Why didn't you answer me when I called you?" I asked.

"I'm listening to my Walkman," said Lenny. "Calm down, okay? What'd you think?"

"Oh," I said, feeling foolish. "I'm sorry. I . . . uh . . . just thought . . . maybe you were upset."

"Upset?" Lenny snorted. "Why? Because you don't want to be bothered with me anymore? Don't flatter yourself, Carver. I don't need friends like you."

That made me feel pretty low, and for a minute I didn't know what to say to him.

"Go on back to bed," he said sarcastically. "And don't worry your pretty little head about me anymore. I'll be fine."

"Look, Lenny," I said, reaching out to touch his arm again.

"Shut up and get out of here," he said, whacking my hand away. "I don't want your sympathy."

"I'm not giving you sympathy, Lenny," I said. "I'd just like to be friends, okay?"

"Yeah, right," he said, "like we were before, huh?"

"Yeah," I said, "like we were before."

There was a silence, then Lenny said quietly, "You mean it?"

"Of course I mean it," I told him. "Look, Lenny. I'm really sorry about the other night. You poured your guts out to me and I stomped on 'em. I can be a real jerk sometimes."

Lenny didn't say anything right away. I guess he wasn't sure he could trust me.

"I mean it, Lenny," I said. "I'd really like to be friends, and if you give me a chance, I'll prove it. What do you say when we get out of here we do some dirt biking together? You ride?"

"No," said Lenny, tentatively, "but I've always wanted to."

"Cool," I said. "I'll teach you."

"No kidding?" Lenny was smiling by then. I could tell by the sound of his voice.

"No kidding," I answered.

"Thanks," said Lenny. "That sounds great." Then he sighed again.

"Now what's wrong?" I asked.

"I'm going home tomorrow," he said quietly.

"Really?"

"Yeah."

"You don't sound too happy," I said.

"No, I'm happy," he said. "I mean, it beats this place, right?"

I laughed. "That's for sure. It'll be lonely here without you, though."

"Ah, you'll be going home in a few days, won't you?"

"I guess so," I said, "depending on how my eye is when they take the bandages off."

"How do you think it is?" asked Lenny.

"Okay, I hope. It doesn't hurt anymore."

"That's cool. Are you gonna be able to see as well as ever?"

My heart sank a little, with worry. "I don't know," I said. "I lost the lens. They're going to fit me with a contact."

Lenny was quiet for a while.

"You're pretty brave about it," he said at last.

I felt tears start in my eyes, and I couldn't answer right away. Finally, I said, "I don't have any choice."

"Yeah," Lenny sighed. "I know the feeling."

"You gonna tell your parents?" I asked.

"I don't know." He sighed again. "Jim wants me to, but I really don't know if I can. It's just such a cruel joke. My parents finally get the son they wished for, and it turns out their 'bonus baby' is a fag."

"Don't call yourself that, Lenny," I said angrily. "Don't ever call yourself that again. You're not a fag, or a queer, or any of those things. Being gay doesn't make you a freak any more than my having one eye makes me one. We're just a couple of kids, okay? Just a couple of regular kids."

"Thanks, Luke," Lenny said quietly. "I know you're trying to help. But it's just not the same thing. Nobody's going to blame you for losing your eye the way they'll blame me for being gay."

I swallowed hard. *"Nobody's going to blame you for losing your eye."* I opened my mouth a little, and the truth was right there and the words almost spilled out, but then I got sort of shaky inside and chickened out.

Maybe I should tell Lenny. Maybe I'd feel better telling somebody. But I don't know. I get shaky again just thinking about it.

Friday, February 21

Well, the good news is, Dr. Hurst said the new lens is working great. She gave me the okay to drive and to go back to school on Monday. The bad news is, Jim really messed with my head today, and now I'm feeling like he's chased me right to the edge of a sheer cliff and there's no way out but down.

I was feeling tense even before I got to the session. Maybe it was thinking about going back to school and facing everybody on Monday. I don't know. I just felt real edgy.

"Have a seat, Luke," Jim said.

"I don't feel like sitting," I told him. "I feel like walking around."

"Well, okay," he said. "Shall we take a walk then?"

"Where?"

"There's a solarium at the end of the hall. Would you like to walk there?"

"Are there other people there?"

"Not usually. Most of the kids prefer to hang out in the rec room."

"Okay," I said. "Let's walk."

Jim led the way out of his office and down the corridor.

"How's your eye coming along?" he asked.

"Good," I said. "I only lost a little bit of peripheral vision up in one corner."

"You were lucky," he said.

My heart did a little skip, like it does every time I think of how lucky I was.

"Yeah," I said quietly.

"You seem agitated today, Luke. Is something wrong?"

I sighed. "I'm tired of all this," I said. "Tired of all the talking and thinking. And I'm starting to feel like a marshmallow. I need to *move*–wrestle, ride, climb a mountain!"

"Do you find that moving helps to keep you from thinking?" Jim asked.

I frowned. "Why? Are you going to twist that into some kind of a problem, too?"

Jim laughed. "I guess that's my job," he said.

"Well, it's a pain in the butt," I told him.

Jim chuckled. "Have you always been so physical?" he asked.

I thought about that. "Yeah," I said. "I'm not good at staying still."

"Your hospitalizations must have been hard on you, then. Retinal surgery involves an extensive recovery period, doesn't it?"

I tensed up immediately. Jim was on a trail again. I could tell.

"So," I said. "What of it?"

Jim smiled. "Don't go getting all defensive on me," he said. "I'm just making conversation."

Yeah, right, I thought. Sniffing out a scent is what you're doing.

"Am I right?" he asked.

"About what?"

"About retinal surgery?"

I sighed. I *was* tired, tired of the questions, tired of running from the truth. Maybe, in a way, I was ready to be caught. I let my mind go, not too far, not too fast, back to those painful memories.

"Yeah," I said quietly. "I was laid up a long time."

"How long?"

"Over a year altogether. It happened the summer before eighth grade, so I wasn't wrestling or playing football yet. I was on a soccer team, though, and I missed that. Most of all, I missed riding my dirt bike and just doing normal kid things. The hardest part was the first couple of weeks after each surgery."

"Because you had to spend those weeks in bed?"

"Because I had to spend them *facedown* in bed."

Jim whistled. "Facedown? How did you breathe?"

I shrugged. "They support your head with cushions and stuff. After a while my parents rigged up a kind of sling."

Jim nodded thoughtfully.

"They put a bubble of gas in your eye," I told him, "to hold the retina in place. You have to keep that bubble pressing against the back of your eye."

"How many times did you have to go through that?" Jim asked.

"Three," I said.

"And then?"

"And then the eye died, from all the trauma, and I had to have it removed and the fake one put in."

"I see," Jim's voice was gentle. "That's . . . a lot for a kid to go through."

My mind soared back and hovered over my bed. My parents had moved it to the family room, so I could be with the family and hear the TV. I saw my body stretched out on it, facedown, staring at nothing, breathing in my own moist breath. I remembered my muscles aching from lying in one position, my skin twitching and itching. I remembered liking the noise of my family around me, hating the long hours alone, when everything was quiet. . . .

"You must have had a lot of thinking time," Jim said. "What did you think about all those days in bed?"

"I don't know," I told him shortly. I called my mind back, recoiling from the pain. "That was a long time ago."

"Yes, Luke," Jim said. "It *was* a long time ago. Maybe it's time to put whatever happened back then to rest, huh?"

He pushed a door open and we walked into the solarium. He steered me over to a window, but the sun was so bright, it bothered my eye. I turned so I could feel it on my back instead. It warmed me on the outside, but inside, I felt hollow and cold.

"Your parents are pretty impressed by the way you handled all the surgery," Jim told me. "They say you never complained. Not once."

I snorted. "Yeah," I said. "I'm a freakin' saint."

"Why are you so down on yourself, Luke?" Jim asked. "Aren't you proud of the way you handled the surgery?"

"Proud?" I shook my head. "I don't see where I had any choice if you want the truth."

There was a silence, and then Jim said quietly, "I *would* like to know the truth, Luke. Would you like to tell it to me?"

This was it, I realized. Jim was closing in for the kill.

Part of me wanted to puff up my feathers and fight, but the other part of me was too damn tired. The *truth*. The God-damn *truth*. It had been weighing me down for a lot of years, and suddenly I didn't feel like I could carry it one more step. The windowsill was wide and low. I sank down onto it.

"Everything I say is confidential, right?" I said.

"Yes. You know it is."

"I mean, you'd never tell my parents anything I tell you without my permission, right?"

"Not unless you plan to do harm to yourself or to someone else, Luke."

I nodded, then leaned to one side and rested my head against the cool, concrete wall. "I lied to them," I said softly. "I've been lying to them for four years."

Jim didn't say anything, but somehow, I got the sense that he'd known this all along.

For the first time in four years, I set my mind free, let it fly without restriction, straight back to the summer when I was thirteen. "What happened to me wasn't an accident," I told Jim. "I'd started hanging with kind of a tough crowd, especially that summer down at the Cape. The other boys were older than me, but because I was so big and looked so much older than I was, they let me hang out with them. I started getting into some stuff I wasn't ready for—cigarettes, alcohol, that sort of thing. My parents had no clue. I'd never been in any real trouble up until then, and they trusted me. The more I got away with, the cockier I got, and pretty soon I was starting to think I didn't have to live by their rules, or anyone else's.

"These guys had formed sort of a gang, and to get into it, you had to fight someone. I wanted to belong, to be a part of it, so one day, while my parents were out shopping, we left the island and went looking for someone for me to fight. We found some boys at the beach across the bay, and I picked a fight with a kid who looked to be about my size. I felt like a real phony doing it, too, because the kid hadn't done anything and I had to make it all up, like he'd given me a dirty look and was looking for trouble, when all he was doing was sitting there minding his own business. I kept after him till he finally got mad, and we arranged to meet behind the local market a half hour later."

"Were you scared?" asked Jim.

"Yeah," I admitted. "I'd never been in that kind of a fight. The ones I'd been in before were nothing more than scuffles in the dirt on the grade-school playground. But this was different. We weren't little kids anymore. We were big enough to really hurt each other. I thought about backing out, but you know how it is. I wanted the guys to accept me, to respect me, so I went.

"The other boys were already waiting when we got there, and they looked pretty eager for the fight. All except the kid I was supposed to fight. He looked just as scared as me. And I was pretty damned scared. My mouth was dry and my gut was in a knot. I was afraid of getting hurt, afraid of getting caught. If someone had yelled 'boo' right then, I probably would have run like hell."

"But you stayed?" said Jim.

I nodded. "The older guys started egging us on. Next

170

thing I knew, they pushed the two of us into the center of the group, and there we were, eye to eye. I remember looking at him and wondering one last time what the hell I was doing there. I wanted to punch him about as much as I wanted leprosy. But by then, all the other guys were shouting and cheering.

"'Hit 'em, Luke!' my friends were yelling. 'C'mon, knock 'em dead! You can do it!'

"So I hit him. And I can still remember the feel of my fist connecting with the bone in his jaw. He let out a grunt, and then blood spurted from his lip. It made me sick. I wanted to stop. But then he punched back and stung me good in the ear, and that made me angry enough to keep going. I jabbed at him a few more times, landing a few glancing blows, and he did the same. Then, next thing I know, he connected with my eye. There was a bright white flash of pain, and I buckled."

"Then what?" asked Jim.

"That was it," I said. "It was over. The other kid got really upset when he saw how bad I was hurt. He came over to apologize. That's the kind of kid he was. I pick a fight with him, hit him first, and he apologizes for hurting me."

"He turned out to be a nice guy, then?"

"Yeah, real nice."

"So, the fight was all for nothing?" said Jim.

"Yes." I felt tears start behind my eyes. "All for nothing."

There was a silence. "And that's the reason for all your stoicism," Jim said at last. "You blame yourself for what happened."

"Yeah," I said, my voice just above a whisper.

"And for everything you and your family have gone through as a result?"

"That's right."

"That's a lot of guilt to carry around."

I swallowed hard but said nothing.

Jim put a hand on my shoulder. "When you think about that day now," he said, "how does it feel?"

"Bad," I said. "How do you expect it to feel?"

Jim shrugged. "Why do you think it feels so bad?"

"Because I knew better. I wasn't raised that way."

There was a long, thoughtful silence, and then Jim said, "Let me ask you a hypothetical question, Luke: What if nothing unusual had happened to you that day? What if you'd gotten into that fight, maybe gotten a black eye, and that was it? How would you feel about the whole thing today?"

I took my time thinking about this. It was something I'd never really considered before. "I still wouldn't be proud of it," I said at last, "but I probably would've pretty much forgotten about it by now."

"Exactly," said Jim.

"What are you getting at?" I asked.

Jim sighed. "Look, Luke," he said. "I'm not condoning fighting. But let's face it, we live in a pretty violent society. I keep hoping we'll get beyond all the macho nonsense someday, but as of right now, most boys still get the message loud and clear that they've got to punch somebody to prove they're a man."

"Are you trying to tell me I'm not responsible for what I did?" I asked.

Jim shook his head. "No. I'm not absolving you from

responsibility," he said. "You knew right from wrong, and you made a bad choice; but I *am* saying that what you did was *understandable.* Understandable and very human, Luke. You have to forgive yourself for being human."

I clenched my teeth together. "You don't understand," I said quietly. "I've been lying to my parents for *four* years."

Jim squeezed my shoulder. "That's an awful burden to have to carry," he said kindly. "You must have felt very lonely at times."

Lonely? Yes. Tears welled in my eyes. I propped my elbows on my knees and leaned forward, resting my chin on my clasped hands.

"Big as we were," I said, "we were still pretty young, and we were all afraid of getting in trouble with our parents. I had no idea how bad I was hurt. There was no blood or anything, and the pain only lasted a few minutes. I figured I'd just have a black eye for a couple of days and that would be it. We came up with the wrestling story so none of us would get punished."

"Sounds like something I might have done at thirteen," Jim said.

"Yeah," I said. "Only I didn't get better. Every day I'd look in the mirror first thing, blinking first one eye, then the other. And each day the image in the mirror grew cloudier. I was frightened. I wanted to tell my parents, but I was scared of them finding out the truth. Besides, one of my friends kept insisting that he'd had a black eye before and it was the same way. I didn't want to look like a wimp, so I kept quiet.

"By the third day I couldn't see at all, and my eye had

turned a funny shade of green. The little black part in the middle wouldn't move either, wouldn't open and close like the one in the other eye. That's when my mother looked at me and noticed something weird."

"What happened then?"

"I can't even remember. It was such a blur. My parents seemed really scared, but at first I still didn't think it could be too bad, because it didn't hurt or anything. I figured they'd take me to the doctor and he'd give me a pill or something, and that would be it. Well, we went to the emergency room, and that's when I started to get nervous, because they kept calling more and more doctors in, and nobody was smiling, and my parents were getting paler and paler. Then they sent us to an eye specialist, and he told us how bad it was and sent us into Boston, to a special hospital for eyes.

"And it just went on that way, from bad to worse. One surgery after another failed, and with each failure the chances for recovery got worse. My parents were like zombies. And through it all they kept saying how unfair it was—how I was such a wonderful, good kid and how something like that shouldn't happen to someone like me."

"And the whole while you kept the truth locked up inside?"

"Yeah. And I knew it was wrong. I kept trying to find a way to tell them, but they were so upset, I couldn't bring myself to hurt them worse. I kept thinking things had to get better, and once they did, it would be easier to tell them."

"But things never got better?"

"No, and by the time it was all over, it had been so

long that there was just . . . no excuse for it. I was too scared by then."

"Scared of what?"

"I don't know." Tears oozed out of my eyes. "Of losing their love, I guess. Of having them realize that I wasn't the great kid they thought I was."

Jim sat down beside me on the windowsill.

"You're being awfully tough on yourself, Luke," he said. "You know, parents really don't expect us to be perfect. They may push us hard and try to help us be the best we can be, but they know we're going to make mistakes. They know because they're human, and they've made mistakes, too."

I looked down at my hands, at the fresh pink scars on my knuckles.

"Not like mine," I said quietly.

Jim chuckled. "Don't be so sure," he said. Then he laughed. "There were a few episodes in my past that I'd just as soon my son never found out about."

I smiled a little, wondering if my parents had secret sins, too.

"Why don't you try telling your parents the truth, Luke?" Jim said. "This lie is really weighing on you, and I don't think you'll ever really be free to move on until you've put it behind you."

Behind me? Of course I'd like to have this lie behind me. But there's a big distance between "ahead of" and "behind," and there's a huge hurdle in between, and I'm just not sure I can get over it.

Wednesday, February 26

I haven't had time to write much. It's been really hectic getting back to school. There's a ton of stuff to catch up on. The first day was kind of hard. I felt like people were staring at me all day long. Things are pretty much back to normal now, though. Except that I still haven't talked to Megan. I want to, but I just don't seem to be able to work up the nerve. Every time I see her heading in my direction, I hide.

I stopped by to see Lenny today. I wanted to tell him about the lie. He was real cool about it. I'm sure it didn't seem like that big of a deal to him compared to the lie he's been hiding, but he didn't act that way. He seemed to really understand how big a deal it was to me.

Believe it or not, Lenny is becoming the best friend I've ever had. Who'da thunk it, huh? If someone had told me, even a couple of months ago, that I'd ever be best friends with a gay guy, I would have told them they were nuts. It's funny how things happen sometimes. I really changed a lot after I got hurt the first time, and I know I'm changing again now, and I think it's for the better. There's got to be an easier way, though. These lessons are killing me.

Thursday, February 27

Wow. The weirdest thing just happened. I've been sitting here for a while, thinking about what Jim said last Friday, and sort of flipping back and forth through my journal, and I came across my poem, "The Falcon." I read it again, and, man, it gave me goose bumps. You know what I just realized? I was writing about *me* in that poem.

I am the falcon!

> *The falcon sits*
> *with his head sagging down*
> *and his eyes staring up,*
> *a chain around his leg.*

Freaky, huh? The lie is the chain that's been keeping me from flying free. And even though I didn't know that back then, somehow the truth came out in my writing. Truth has a way of doing that, I've noticed, sneaking into your writing.

I guess it's time I faced the truth, time I broke this chain and learned to fly. And I know, deep inside, that Jim is right about my parents. They'll be there, arms out, waiting to catch me if I fall. Just like they've always been.

But still, that first step is going to be a doozy.

Saturday, March 1

I've been trying for the last couple of days to work up the nerve to tell my parents about the lie, but I keep chickening out. Lenny says he's been having the same trouble ever since he got out of the hospital. So this morning I got this idea. I went over to see him, and we made a pact. We're both going to tell our parents this afternoon, at three o'clock, and then we're going to get together tonight to help each other pick up the pieces. I still have butterflies about it, but it makes it easier somehow, knowing that Lenny is going through the same thing. We talked for a long time this morning, and I felt stronger when I left, stronger than I've felt in a long time. I even worked up the courage to stop by and see Megan on the way home. She was out back with her horse again when I pulled into her driveway. She looked surprised to see me.

"Hey," she called. "Long time, no see."

I grimaced, and then she blushed bright red.

"Oh jeez," she said, clapping a hand over her mouth. "I didn't mean it like that. I . . ."

I smiled as I walked toward her. "It's okay," I said. "Pretty good pun, actually."

Megan smiled, too. "Let me try again," she said. "How about, what brings you here?"

I shrugged, then stuffed my hands in my pockets. "Just wanted to talk to you," I said.

"It's about time," she said quietly.

Her horse gave a sudden loud snort, and I jumped back.

Megan laughed. "Don't worry," she said. "He doesn't bite."

"I don't know," I said. "Horses scare me."

Megan's brow furrowed. "Horses scare you?" she said. "And dirt bikes don't?"

"Dirt bikes don't have minds of their own," I told her.

"Ah." Megan raised her eyebrows. "And is that what scared you about me, too?"

I could feel myself blushing. "No," I said. "I liked that about you."

Megan gave me a skeptical eye, then went back to brushing. "Well, what was it then?" she asked.

I hesitated for a minute, but I was done with hiding the truth, done with keeping my feelings a secret—even from myself. "I think . . . I was afraid I was falling in love with you," I said.

Megan stopped with her brush in midair and looked at me. She slowly lowered her arm. "So what?" she said softly. "I was falling in love with you, too."

A lump rose up in my throat, and I swallowed it down. "I know," I said. "I was afraid of that, too."

Megan's eyes searched mine. "Why?" she asked.

"I don't know." I looked down and kicked at a rock. "I've still got college and all . . ."

Megan put her brush down and came over to me. "Luke," she said, smiling gently, "believe it or not, I've got a life, too. And a lot of plans. College, vet school, a clinic of my own, and maybe . . . someday . . . marriage and a family. But that's a long way off. I'm not thinking that far ahead. Right now, I'm just thinking that I like you, more than any other guy I've ever known. And that's all. Okay?"

I heard everything she said, but I heard one part extra loud and clear: "I like you, *more than any other guy* . . ."

"Even more than Tony?" I asked.

Megan looked puzzled. "Even more than Tony, what?" she returned.

"You like *me* more than Tony?" I repeated.

She shook her head and smiled. "Tony and I are just friends," she said. "I've told you that from the beginning."

My heart gave a little leap. So, old Tony *had* been stretching the truth. I couldn't help smiling to myself.

"What are you grinning about?" asked Megan.

For a moment I thought of telling her about Tony, exposing him for what he was. But then, when I really thought about it, I realized that what old Tony probably was, was human. And I guessed if I could forgive myself for being human, I could forgive Tony, too.

"Nothing," I said, grinning wider.

She gave me a funny smile then, and suddenly I wanted to kiss her more than anything. So I did. And then she put her arms around my neck and kissed me back. I mean really *kissed* me. Then I held her, just held her for the longest time.

When she pulled back and looked at me again, her eyes were wet. "Welcome back, Luke Carver," she whispered. "Where have you been?"

I looked down. "It's a long story," I said quietly.

She tilted my chin up with her hand and looked deeply, steadily, into my eyes.

"Luke," she said gently, "I've got time."

And she's right. We do have time.

But I don't.

The clock downstairs in the front hall is chiming three, and my heart is lurching with every bong. Part of me wants to chicken out again, but I know, across town, Lenny's heart is lurching, too, and he's counting on me like I'm counting on him. So, I guess this is it. The edge of the cliff.

Deep breath.

Wings out.

Geronimo!